POSSESSED

THE OUIJA BOARD

MAHTAB NARSIMHAN

POSSESSED : THE OUIJA BOARD

EERIE TALES FROM THE EAST : BOOK 3

Copyright © 2022 by Mahtab Narsimhan

All rights reserved.

No part of this book may be reproduced in any form or by any electronic or mechanical means, including information storage and retrieval systems, without written permission from the author, except for the use of brief quotations in a book review.

For more information, go to:

www.mahtabnarsimhan.com

Cover Design by PINTADO

Book Design by Mahtab Narsimhan

Published by Stardust Stories

ISBN PRINT BOOK: 978-1-7778318-5-1

First Edition: June 2022

For all those who love scary stories

PROLOGUE

The boy huddled behind a tombstone, trying not to sob. He took in a ragged breath, goosebumps exploding on his skin. It was only the end of August and the California nights had been cooler, but far from chilly. Tonight, however, felt like the middle of winter, in *Canada*. All around the graveyard, shadows flickered without the slightest hint of wind.

Panic flooded the boy as he debated with himself. *Why did I agree to do this?* He didn't need to be in this group. He had friends—*good* friends. Sort of. What had he been thinking when he'd said yes to this dare?

"Hey, what's the hold-up?" a voice called out in the distance. "If you're too scared, just say so. Quit wasting our time."

A gust of wind swept icy raindrops down his neck. He shivered and leaped to his feet, making up his mind. The boys had dared him to race to the center of the graveyard, touch the ancient crypt, and come back to the gates, where they waited—an initiation that had sounded painless, at first.

"Yeah, come on back if you want and we'll go home," said another boy in a hollow voice. "No one's forcing you to do this." Muffled laughter echoed in the mist.

He *could* do this. He was going to do it! He just had to be brave for a few minutes and he'd be in. Surely that couldn't be too hard? And then no one would say he was a coward.

The boy gulped, swallowing the lump of fear lodged in his throat, and took off. Blood, and the sound of his own footsteps, pounded in his ears as he ran, dodging tombstones and open graves. The globe lights atop lamp posts shed watery light along the path that led to the crypt. As he approached, a stink of rotting leaves rose up in the air. There was something else, too, something putrid. A dying animal? A skunk? He covered his nose and mouth with his arm and hurried on.

An iron fence with a latched gate enclosed the crypt: a dark, squat square of brick. The cold metal of the gate seared the boy's fingertips. Every instinct screamed at him, *Run! Forget this initiation and get out of here.*

Only pride and a deep desire to join the cool kids made him walk into the enclosure. The dread in his heart ballooned as winged shadows flitted past his face, making him whimper. The bats stank of damp fur and urine. Still the boy approached the crypt, his breath fogging in front of his face. He reached out an arm, which shook so badly, he felt as if he had the flu.

But under his palm, the brick was warm. Pleasantly so. The boy breathed deeply.

I did it!

Nothing had jumped out of the crypt or crawled out of the cavernous entrance. The mist hung as it did before, almost seeming friendlier. Letting his shoulders fall back, he made a mental note: Reality was less scary than your imagination. All you had to do was see something right through to the end. He tried to smile, but his face wouldn't cooperate.

The grand realization sank in. Now that he'd completed the task, he was part of *the* group. Not only would he never be lonely again at school, but he would also have a place at the cool kids' table. *Him!* Relief and adrenaline made the boy bolder.

He stared at the crypt and slapped a hand on it. "You're just an old, useless pile of bricks and I'm not scared of you."

Nothing happened and, feeling braver, the boy gave it a swift kick. "There! That's for scaring me—"

A sharp current jolted him from head to toe. It felt as if someone were ripping him apart and climbing into him. He couldn't scream or breathe. His limbs seemed paralyzed, and his skin seemed to be on fire.

What was happening to him? *Help!* the boy screamed silently as the world momentarily turned dark.

As suddenly as the sensation had started, it stopped. The boy gasped for air and took in a shuddering breath as the graveyard came back into focus. His head pounded, his lungs were fit to burst, and his mouth was dry.

Were the others playing tricks on him? Was it someone else? How . . . ? He scanned the surroundings. The gravestones looked back at him silently, offering no explanation. Only the shadows shivered in the wind. As soon as he regained command of his feet, the boy raced back to the gate, where the gang stood.

"So?" one of them asked.

"P-piece of cake," the boy replied.

Everyone gathered around him, thumping his back and punching him playfully.

"Welcome to the club," another said.

But the boy barely heard him. Inside his head, someone was cackling like a maniac.

1

How did I get so lucky to have not one but two best friends in the world? thought Michiko. So why couldn't she confide in them?

"Penny for your thoughts?" said Sophia, tossing back a mass of wavy black hair as she glanced at the cafeteria door over her shoulder.

"I'd go up to a dollar," said Kate. Her green eyes, boring into Michiko, were tinged with concern. "Is something bothering you? You know we're always here for you, right?"

"Ditto," added Sophia with a wink. "You know I got your back, girl."

Michiko nodded, swallowing the lump in her throat. These two were the absolute best and yet . . . she couldn't tell them the secret she'd been keeping for months.

Just then Lucas walked by. Kate and Sophia immediately fell silent as their eyes followed the new boy in their Grade 8 class. Tall, blonde, and blue-eyed, Lucas oozed swagger, even though he'd just started here in September. It seemed to Michiko that her best friends were crushing on the popular kid, too. As far as she was concerned, though, he was just... *meh*.

"Should we join them?" asked Kate, curling a lock of brown hair around her finger as the object of her attention plunked himself down at the packed table next to theirs.

"We should get him to sit with *us*," said Sophia, not taking her eyes off him.

"Hey, Lucas, Sasha," a voice called out, "mind if I join you? All the other tables are full."

Michiko didn't turn around. She knew that voice. From Kate's and Sophia's grimaces, they recognized the high pitch too. Sadia Siddiqui—only the most irritating girl in their class—slid into the seat across from Lucas without waiting for his response.

Michiko exchanged glances with Kate and Sophia. Without saying a word, Michiko knew what they were all thinking. Sadia wasn't afraid to show she craved Lucas's company. From the day he'd arrived, she'd tried to find excuses to spend time with him. It infuriated Kate and Sophia but not enough to make them equally pushy. The three rolled their eyes in unison.

There were plenty of open spots in the cafeteria, so Sadia wasn't fooling anyone with her lies. Yet *she* was at the table with Lucas, Sasha, Chadwick, and Irfan—while her friends weren't. If only she could do something to help Kate and Sophia. Something that would make Lucas take notice of the two of them and see how much cooler they were than his gaggle of fans.

"Hi Sadia," Lucas replied. "What's up?"

"What else? I'm excited about our class trip!" Sadia replied, munching on a golden fry.

"The Mojave National Preserve?" drawled Sasha. "Sand, rocks, trees... yawn."

Sophia and Kate were eavesdropping, but Michiko's mind had wandered back to her usual worry. How was Mom feeling right this minute? Had she eaten anything, or was she still sleeping the day away?

"We could have asked Lucas to join us when he walked by," said Sophia, her face glum. "You both would have helped, right?"

"Umm . . . do we want to look that desperate?" said Kate.

"That's just called being friendly, right, Michiko?" asked Sophia but got no answer. "Earth to Michiko! Are you *sure* everything's okay?"

"Wha . . . oh, sure!" said Michiko, pasting on a smile and hoping her friends wouldn't probe any more. "Hey, we should decide what we're bringing on the trip. It'll be two days and *two whole nights*, almost like an extended sleepover! Plus, we'll be roomies. Shall we pack something fun to do in the evenings?"

Loud laughter from the next table made them all look. Sadia was laughing as if she'd heard the funniest thing in her life. Lucas was smiling. Sasha looked bored, which seemed to be his default expression.

"Wish we could do something to get into Lucas's group," mumbled Sophia.

"Yeah, this trip will be make or break, I can feel it," said Kate. "By the end of it, either we're in or we're still out." She paused. "I just wish we knew *what* to do to win him over. Should we get bolder or keep playing it cool?"

"Should we ask my Magic 8 Ball?" Sophia smirked.

"Nah, this might be a job for a crystal ball," said Kate with a sigh.

"Kokkuri-san!" Michiko spoke up without preamble. "I mean, Kokkuri-san is the answer to all our problems." She had long been meaning to bring up the topic and here was her chance. "The trip is the perfect time to play."

"Umm ... who?" asked Kate.

"Play what?" said Sophia.

Michiko gestured for them to huddle, even though the din in the cafeteria would have made it impossible for anyone to eavesdrop. "In Japan, one just asks Kokkuri-san—a spirit who comes when summoned, answers all questions, and leaves. It's like the Ouija board."

Kate paled; her green eyes wide. Sophia's thick eyebrows knitted together as she stared at Michiko, looking thoughtful.

These were the exact reactions she'd been expecting—and Michiko knew she'd have to press harder. Kate and Sophia were usually game to try new things, so why not this too? She *had* to convince them; in fact, she had no other choice.

"Well?"

"I've heard ... umm ... terrible things about Ouija board summonings gone wrong," said Kate almost in a whisper. "Like when the spirit refuses to leave and haunts the people who called it? Sometimes for as long as they live." She rubbed the goosebumps on her arms, blinking rapidly. "No way."

"But Kokkuri-san is different," insisted Michiko. "A mix between a fox, a dog, and a raccoon, Kokkuri-san is an *animal* spirit. Each time you call, it's a different aspect of those animals that manifests itself. Surely, you're not scared of cute animals, right, Kate?"

She said nothing, her eyes darting to Sophia.

"What if Kokkuri-san told you which of you had a chance with Lucas? And how to get into his group?"

"Ooh! Have you done this before?" asked Sophia, her

curious gaze locked on Michiko. "Summoned this spirit with a Ouija board?"

"Wait, seriously?" Kate frowned before adding, "Have you?"

Now this was a gray area. Michiko had been part of a summoning loads of times with her cousins in Japan—though she'd never summoned the spirit on her own. If she glossed over that detail, they would play. And she *needed* them to play because this game just wouldn't work with one person. Two was the minimum and three was best. Also, it had to be played with people you trusted. Michiko's mind whirled as she cringed inside. She trusted Kate and Sophia with her life, and yet she was about to lie to her best friends. The irony did not escape her.

"Yes or no, Michiko?" asked Kate. "It's a simple question."

"Yes," replied Michiko simply, squashing her guilt. To herself, she added, *I'm doing this for her.*

"When did you ever use the Ouija board to summon this Ko thingy?" pressed Kate.

Michiko stared back at Kate. She was timid—she could make a puppy look ferocious—but her mind was razor-sharp. "It's Kokkuri-san, and the name means "to nod." I played it when I was in Japan last year. It was easy and fun. And we got some excellent answers and made the right choices, thanks to the spirit's help."

"I'll save you a seat on the bus tomorrow, Lucas," Sadia's shrill voice interrupted them, again, just as the bell signaled the end of lunch break.

Michiko looked over at the other table, where Lucas sat with a curiously glazed expression on his face, as if he were here, yet far away. His pepperoni pizza, which smelled a bit stale—she'd always had a *very* sensitive nose—was untouched. Michiko mentally chided him for being so wasteful, even with food that didn't seem too appetizing. Mom would have had a fit if that were her plate.

Mom.

"So?" asked Michiko, snapping back to the present and getting to her feet. "You guys in or out?"

"In," said Sophia. "I have a question or two I'd like to ask about Lucas—and that *cucaracha* Sadia."

"That's the spirit!" said Michiko with a laugh, though her heart was thumping hard.

Sophia flashed her a cheeky grin. "Nice one!"

Kate said nothing, but Michiko knew she would play, eventually. That's what Michiko was counting on—that her best friends would come through for her.

Walking down the bustling corridor, the three kept gabbing about all the answers they would have by the end of this trip. If Sadia could get any worse, if Lucas would finally be their friend, if one of them had a real chance with him, if they'd ever be dubbed the popular kids . . . Only Michiko couldn't speak aloud the one answer she was desperate for.

2

The chatter in the classroom died away as soon as their homeroom teacher, Ms. Fraser, walked in. Petite, with flaming red hair and deep brown eyes, she was strict but fair. Everyone in Grade 8 loved her.

"Are we ready for the class trip tomorrow?" she asked, her gaze sweeping the classroom. "I have some last-minute instructions, so listen up. Visiting the Mojave National Preserve is an amazing opportunity to learn about our environment and climate change. We'll have fun, but I ask you all to be respectful of the surroundings and listen to our guides. As you already know, there are snakes and other dangers, and I'd rather not have to call your parents, or an ambulance. Clear? Now..."

Michiko barely listened. She was busy scribbling a list of everything she would need to summon Kokkuri-san.

1. A piece of paper with letters and numbers (plus YES, NO, and the red torii gate drawn at the top)
2. A ten-yen coin (from my last visit to Japan)

3. Two volunteers (with courage and common sense)

"Michiko!" A voice broke through her exercise, and she startled.

"Yes, Ms. Fraser?" she said.

"You aren't paying attention," the teacher replied. "What's going on?"

All eyes were on her, and Michiko felt her face go warm. She didn't like being in the spotlight, especially for not paying attention.

"I was making a list of what to bring tomorrow," said Michiko. "I'm just so excited." This was the partial truth, and hopefully Ms. Fraser would not ask to see it.

"Good," said Ms. Fraser, "but you already have my list of what you need to bring. I'd rather you paid attention to the instructions now. They are about keeping you all safe. Okay?"

Michiko nodded, annoyed that the teacher had to single her out. Sadia was playing tic-tac-toe with a friend. Others were doodling. Why pick on *her* and not them? *Unfair!*

"Bring your overnight bags to school with you," Ms. Fraser continued. "We'll work most of Wednesday morning and leave after lunch. Your parents will pick you up from the school parking lot on Friday evening. Also, carry layers so you can dress warmly. I've been told the end of October can bring unpredictable weather to the preserve. Lastly, the bus leaves at two tomorrow. If you're not on it, we leave you behind and you miss out on a wonderful trip. Now, books out, please!"

For the rest of the afternoon, they worked on math and geography in their homeroom. Michiko's stomach quivered with excitement at the thought of the trip, but for different reasons. Though she'd been too inexperienced to lead the summoning of Kokkuri-san when she and her cousins had played, she knew exactly how it was done. Putting it into practice shouldn't be too hard.

Finally, the bell rang, signaling the end of day. Everyone jumped up, crammed books into bags, and hurried out of class. Michiko, Sophia, and Kate walked home together down their regular route.

"So . . . we *sure* we want to do this?" Kate asked as they turned a corner. "I'm having second thoughts. We'll be away from home, so if we're in trouble, we can't even ask for help. I just get a bad feeling—"

"Don't you want a chance to see into the future?" asked Michiko. "Most people would give anything to know." *Like me.*

Sophia slung an arm each around Kate and Michiko. "Relax, Kate—Michiko's done it loads of times! You sure you don't have any stubborn spirits still stuck on you?"

"Only you two," said Michiko while cringing inwardly.

They both had a point, even if they didn't know it. That the spirit was not always a benign trickster. Also capable of malevolence, Kokkuri-san could indeed possess players, drive them mad, and refuse to leave if summoned incorrectly—Michiko had heard the rumors. She made a note to be extra careful, follow her cousin Hiro's steps to a T, and stop at the first sign of trouble. Yet the weight of the knowledge only she was privy to settled deep in her gut. She knew this game was not to be played lightly; she also knew what was at stake here.

What she didn't know was an answer only Kokkuri-san could provide.

Is Mom going to die?

3

The two-and-a-half-hour bus ride took almost four, thanks to the bumper-to-bumper Wednesday traffic from LA to Barstow. From there, it was another hour to the Mojave National Preserve.

At first, there was a lot of chatter on board, which died down as their bus slowed to a crawl. Michiko sat with Sophia and Kate and watched while they scrolled through their phones, cyber-stalking Lucas.

"Can't find anything about him online," said Kate. "Very odd, given that he's so popular."

"Ooooh," said Sophia, "handsome *and* mysterious."

"More like he's hiding something," said Kate. "I mean who's *not* online these days?"

Michiko's thoughts played on loop behind her vacant eyes: Mom's pale face, her relentless hacking cough, the doctor's tight mouth as he explained he was running out of options. Mom's lips had felt papery on Michiko's skin when she'd kissed her goodbye that morning. Three days without her would be tough, but at least she would return to her with an answer. Kokkuri-san would tell her what to do.

POSSESSED

"Why so quiet, girl?" said Sophia. "You better tell us what's bothering you, or I'm stopping the bus right now." Her black eyes glinted wickedly.

"I'll help her!" said Kate.

Michiko couldn't help but smile. Why was she being so stubborn about keeping this from those who loved her? *Because saying it aloud makes it real.* And while she could use the support, she wasn't sure she could handle the concerned looks, the regular check-ins, the public knowledge of her awful reality. No, she would explain *after* they'd spoken to Kokkuri-san. They would know once she asked the question anyway. And they would forgive her silence. She was sure of that.

"Couldn't sleep again last night, you know how it's been," Michiko offered another white lie. "I'm good." Luckily, they believed her this time, too, going back to scouring the net for news about Lucas.

It was evening by the time they arrived. Even though there was no accommodation for the public available at the preserve, the management had made exceptions for school visits and provided lodging at the Kelso Depot, in the heart of the preserve.

As soon as Michiko stepped out of the air-conditioned bus, hot air blasted her face. Though it was only 75 degrees Fahrenheit according to her phone, it felt a lot hotter. Scrub, red rock, and cacti surrounded the depot on all sides. The air smelled of dry earth mixed with something sweet, which she couldn't identify. The horizon was a shimmering haze.

Ms. Fraser herded them all indoors, where the temperature dropped a couple of degrees. They were twenty students in all and three to a room. Two unfortunate students had to share a room with Ms. Fraser. Thankfully, Sophia, Kate, and Michiko had put in a request long ago that they be roomies. This is what had given Michiko the idea to summon the spirit in the first place. They would be together here, but far from interruptions by parents or siblings.

The ranger assigned to their group was a chatty woman called Casey, who would be their guide throughout their stay. She had an infectious laugh and was extremely knowledgeable about the desert and its history, having been here for almost six years. Within the first ten minutes, they got a tour of the lodge, as well as a few warnings.

"No wandering out at night," said Casey. "The preserve has lots of wildlife, including two of the most venomous snakes in the US. The Mojave green is highly toxic, so be vigilant. Make sure you shut the screen door when you leave or enter. We would rather the outdoors stay *outside*." She paused, before adding cheerily, "Any questions?"

"Do you keep an antidote on hand?" Sadia asked. "In case we get bitten?"

"Yes, but we haven't needed to use it in all the years I've been here." Casey looked serious. "And I hope I don't have to for another six."

Everyone was subdued. Kate's eyes flicked around the room nervously. Michiko slipped a hand into her friend's and squeezed. Kate gave her a grateful smile and squeezed back.

Casey clapped for their attention. "No need to look so glum. Snakes and, for that matter, *all* wildlife want as little to do with humans as we want with them. If you respect their space, they'll leave you alone."

"When do the snakes come out?" Karim asked. He was an outdoor enthusiast, even though he looked like he spent all day indoors, in front of a TV.

"Mostly at night, when the place cools down, which is why you all need to stay indoors after dark. So no one will wander around outside after lights-out, right? I need everyone's word."

Her gaze swept the group, and Michiko nodded with the rest.

"Good. Okay, unpack, freshen up, and meet us at the cafeteria," said Casey. "We have a delicious spread for you."

The group split up. Michiko was starving despite the snacks and sandwiches they'd eaten on the way here.

Sophia rubbed her belly and groaned, "I could eat an elephant!"

"No, thanks, I'll just take a burger," said Kate, who was vegetarian.

"I wouldn't mind tasting snake," said Michiko, laughing at the horror on Kate's face.

"Ooooh, that sounds yum," said Sophia, catching on.

"You're both disgusting," said Kate, plugging her ears.

They found the room assigned to them, threw their bags on the beds, and washed up, giggling and teasing each other the entire time. Michiko was able to stop worrying about Mom for a little while, and that felt good. Within minutes, they were in the cafeteria with the rest of the group, where the staff had prepared a simple but delicious buffet. There was something for everyone. Michiko piled her plate with mushroom rice, grilled fish, and veggies. Sophia helped herself to some chicken, while Kate had the plant-based burger and the same sides.

Luckily, this time there was plenty of room at the table where Lucas and Sasha sat. Sadia, unsurprisingly, was there too, as if stuck to them with superglue. Exchanging sideways glances with the two, Michiko marched straight to that table and plunked herself down. Kate and Sophia took seats beside her.

"Hey," said Michiko coolly.

"Hey back," said Lucas, pushing food around his plate, which looked untouched.

Sasha, who had a humongous pile of food on his plate and was shoveling it down as if it might disappear if he wasn't quick enough, acknowledged them with a nod.

"You aren't hungry?" asked Sophia, cutting into a chicken breast.

"Nah," said Lucas, dropping his fork. "I had some snacks on the way. If I get hungry at night, I'll just sneak into the kitchen and grab something."

That got a snort out of Sasha—and a healthy smattering of chewed-up food on the table.

"Gross!" Michiko and Kate said together.

"Guys!" yelled Karim behind them. "Listen to this. The Kelso Depot once had engines to push the trains up the Cima Dome. And Casey said we'll have time to see those!" Karim had probably memorized every detail about the Mojave National Preserve.

"Meh. I'd rather see the Mojave green," said Lucas, leaning forward. At this proximity, his blue eyes had an odd shine to them. "Imagine how cool *that* would be, to see a live and *very* poisonous snake up close."

Kate squeaked softly. Sophia's eyebrows almost disappeared into her hairline. Michiko shivered involuntarily.

"You're fearless, man!" said Sasha and fist-bumped Lucas.

"What's there to fear?" said Lucas.

"Only its venom," said Karim. "Remember what Casey said?"

POSSESSED

Lucas shrugged. *Was he really this reckless, or was he just showing off in front of the others? The latter* thought Michiko.

As the evening sky turned darker, the lights came on in the cafeteria. Almost everyone had finished dinner, and the chatter was loud and lively. Karim yawned, which set everyone else off. Michiko, who was watching the clock, was keen to go back to the room. She caught Kate's and Sophia's eyes and jerked her head toward the cafeteria door.

Sophia took a last bite of dessert and wiped her mouth, not showing any signs of moving. Kate looked away immediately and picked up her phone. *This is going to be an uphill battle*, thought Michiko. They had both said yes to playing the game, and she wouldn't let them back out now.

"There's something special I want you all to hear before bed," said Casey finally, silencing the group. "Follow me."

Chairs scraped the wooden floor as they stood up as one and followed Casey to the main door. She switched on the lights outside and stomped on the ground, eyes searching the shadows. "All clear—no snakes," she said.

Once they were all outside, Casey switched off the lights. Michiko huddled together with her classmates, shivering as the cold air swept over her skin. What a difference a few hours had made. A sickle moon lit the landscape and, for a few seconds, there was perfect silence.

Then they heard it—a buzzing sound in the distance. It sounded like someone was playing a wind instrument . . . underground. The hair on the back of Michiko's neck prickled. It sounded ghostly.

"What is that?" a classmate asked.

"I-is this place haunted?" Kate said in a whisper.

"It's the singing dunes, of course!" piped up Karim. "Ms. Fraser told us about them, remember?"

Michiko didn't remember and, by the annoyed looks on

many faces, neither did her classmates. If Karim didn't shut up about his trivia, he would soon be banned from opening his mouth—and making the rest of them look bad.

Casey laughed. "You're right, Karim. The dunes are a miracle of nature, and tomorrow we'll see why. It's a phenomenal sight. Goodnight, all!"

4

"Dinner and a show—that was awesome!" Sophia flopped onto the bed and rubbed her stomach. "I'm *sooo* sleepy."

"Me too," said Kate, peeling off her socks and climbing into bed. "I just remembered one more place I hadn't thought to look for news on Lucas." She started tapping on her phone.

Michiko quickly texted Mom and Dad in the family group chat to wish them goodnight and let them know she was fine. Dad responded immediately. Nothing from Mom, who was probably asleep. Dad confirmed that seconds later, telling her not to worry and to enjoy herself—which made her all the more determined to summon Kokkuri-san tonight.

"Um, aren't you forgetting the plan?" said Michiko, looking pointedly at Kate and Sophia getting ready to go to bed.

"Let's watch *Titanic* again!" said Sophia. "I can stream it on my phone."

"No!" said Kate and Michiko in unison. "We've watched it . . . like *ten* times already," Michiko added.

"So, what's an eleventh time?" said Sophia, a goofy look on her face. "That Leonardo is so dreamy, and we all love old movies."

Laughing, Kate threw a pillow at Sophia and continued scrolling on her phone.

These two were like her cousin's golden retriever puppy, distracted by anything and everything. Sighing, Michiko decided to set up the board and then call them to join. She opened her backpack and pulled out a clear plastic bag, trying to ignore the irritation creeping up inside. Her friends had no idea why this was so important to her, so she really couldn't blame them for being so distracted, after all.

The bag had everything she needed to summon Kokkuri-san: the "board" she'd sketched on a large piece of paper, neatly folded, as well as the ten-yen coin. She unfolded the paper and placed it on the carpet in the center of the room. At the top of the paper was a red symbol—the torii gate. On either side of it were the words, YES and NO. Under that, evenly spaced out, were the letters of the alphabet, which the spirit would use to spell out the answers. The red of the gate stood out beside the black letters, like a smear of blood. Michiko suppressed a shiver. Until today, she'd only been a sidekick. Now she was the star of the show.

Through the open window, covered by wire mesh, sounds of the night wafted in: the eerie hooting of an owl, a faint rattling and slithering through dry brush, the sinister buzzing of the singing dunes. Michiko tuned it all out and focused on the board, on her task at hand. She had to summon the spirit, ask questions respectfully, and send it back to wherever it came from.

Michiko knew the question about her mother's illness would come as a surprise to Kate and Sophia, but she was going to ask it anyway. It was the whole reason she'd suggested this game. Truth be told, she couldn't care less about Lucas and his group. Not when her mother had been ill for months and the doctors still could not figure out what was wrong with her. She knew her friends were going to be mad at her, but it was a risk she had to take. Every time she'd wanted to confide in them in the past months, something had stopped her. It was as if saying it aloud would make her mother *more* ill. It was totally illogical, she knew, but she couldn't bring herself to say a word to either of them about how worried she'd been. That would all change tonight, and she would have to come clean after all.

"I'm ready," said Michiko, her heart thudding as she gazed from the torii gate to the coin. In a few minutes she'd be summoning a spirit from another world. *Was she up to it? What if she made a mess of it?* She pushed those thoughts away, trying to channel confidence. Her safety . . . *no, her friends' safety*, depended on it.

"Still can't find anything on Lucas," said Kate disgustedly, throwing her phone on the bed. "Can we play this game tomorrow? I'm beat." She yawned widely, as if to prove a point.

"What she said," Sophia piped in. "Let's play tomorrow. I'm sure Ms. Fraser will give us the evening off, and it's not like we can go shopping or to a movie out here in this desert."

Michiko took a deep breath, trying to stay calm. The memory of Mom, whipping up her fave chocolate brownies in the kitchen, flitted through her head. What she wouldn't do to see Mom back on her feet again! "I thought Lucas was starting to get friendlier with us during dinner. Don't you want to know if either of you have a shot at being his . . . um . . . special friend?"

Kate sat up, her eyes wide. "You think so?"

"Michiko has a point," said Sophia. "Or we might just find out we're wasting our time and move on."

A burst of muffled laughter distracted them from their discussion, and they raced to the window as one. A shadow zipped by, and then another. A couple of students were outside, even though Casey had warned them to stay indoors.

"Who was that?" said Sophia. "Why are they outside?"

"Umm . . . Lucas and Sasha," said Kate. "I recognized their hoodies. Especially Lucas's. It's a nice bright orange." She turned to face them. "He's sweet, but not very smart, is he?"

Michiko had to agree as she sat back down, biting her lip. The desert was dangerous at night, Casey had told them more than once. There were other dangers besides snakes. It was getting cooler by the second, and their hoodies wouldn't be warm enough if they got lost and had to spend the night outdoors. *Their problem for being foolish*, she told herself.

"Forget them and come on *already*," Michiko said aloud. Her hands were clammy, and her heart was racing. She knew this could go well or horribly wrong, but she would see it through. She *had* to. For Mom's sake. If Kokkuri-san revealed what was wrong with her mother and how they could make her better, she could phone Dad tonight and tell him.

"Let's do this!" said Sophia, plunking down beside Michiko to study the board. "Come on, Kate," she said, patting the spot beside her.

"Okay," said Kate softly, sitting cross-legged across from her and completing the circle. She still sounded uncertain. "You sure you know what you're doing, Michiko? This won't be dangerous, right?"

POSSESSED

"I'm sure, Kate," said Michiko, getting up to switch off the lights. "Stop being such a worrywart and toughen up." The bedside lamp threw buttery light over the board on the floor, the black letters and numbers standing out.

"We ready?" said Sophia brightly, once the circle was whole again.

Michiko nodded and began. "Here's how it works. Each of us puts one finger on this coin, which starts out at the torii gate. *I* will call out to Kokkuri-san. When the spirit arrives, and it's usually female, the coin will move to YES. It might stink a bit, like rotten seaweed. Then we each ask a question. If the spirit seems friendly, we can go for one more round of questions, after which I can send it back to where it came from. When the spirit leaves, it will say YES again, and the coin will go back to the torii gate. We mustn't keep it for too long in this world—that's very important." She paused. "The longer it stays, the harder it is to send back."

Sophia nodded seriously, flicking her long black hair off her shoulders.

"But what if it *stays* and possesses one of us, like in the movies?" asked Kate in a hushed voice.

Michiko and Sophia exchanged a glance and burst into giggles at the same time.

"This is not like the movies, and I've got you," said Michiko, squeezing her friend's hand. "There's a good chance no one will even show up. Sometimes this spirit is simply not interested in answering questions, in which case we say goodnight and go to sleep. Just do as I say. One last thing—no matter what you do, don't remove your finger from the coin until the spirit has gone back. Clear?"

She swept her gaze from Kate to Sophia, who both whispered yeses.

"So, shall we start?" asked Michiko.

Both nodded, though Kate's smile was tentative. They all reached out their index fingers and touched the cool metal coin. The wind howled outside as Michiko cleared her throat and, with her heart slamming against her ribcage, called out for the trickster spirit.

5
———

"Kokkuri-san, are you here?" The minutes ticked by while Michiko repeated her request. "Please answer me if you have arrived."

"Umm, looks like no one's home," said Kate, sounding almost cheerful. "Can we sleep now?"

Just then Sophia let out a humongous yawn but said nothing. Michiko wanted to scream in frustration. When her cousins in Japan had played the game, it had often worked. Kokkuri-san answered within the first minute or so. *Why couldn't she hear her now? Was she doing it wrong?* Staring at her friends' faces, Michiko couldn't deny that doing it and observing it were very different. *Will I miss my shot at saving Mom?*

She ignored Kate's suggestion to call it a day. This *had* to work. She might not get another chance again, and by that time it might be too late.

"Kokkuri-san, are you here?" asked Michiko, her voice shaking ever so slightly. "Please answer me if you are!" Her throat closed up and tears pricked her eyes, but she waited for a sign.

Sophia cleared her throat. "Michiko, I don't think anyone is listen—"

The coin shifted ever so slightly from the torii gate. The air in the room grew chilly, their breath fogging in front of their faces.

Kate and Sophia were staring at Michiko, wonder and a question in their eyes. She nodded and focused on the board. Her heart was pounding so hard, she thought it might burst out of her chest. Mixed with the fear was joy. She'd led a summoning for the very first time.

"Remember, no matter what, *do not* remove your finger from the coin," said Michiko. Hers was slippery with sweat as it rested between Sophia's brown and Kate's white fingers. They watched as the coin inched across the board and came to rest on the word YES.

Michiko took in a deep breath. "Thank you, Kokkuri-san. We have our first question. Go ahead, Kate."

Kate swallowed and licked her lips, her eyes darting wildly around the room, at the board, and away again. Michiko nodded at her encouragingly. Sophia didn't seem quite as nervous and was studying the board intently. *Good*, thought Michiko.

"Umm . . . K-san, whom among his classmates does Lucas love?" asked Kate. Her face shone with sweat despite the room being cold. She shrugged when she saw Michiko's frown, whispering, "I prefer the short form."

The coin did not move.

"Maybe the spirit doesn't know . . . or it just won't tell us," Kate said, frowning.

"Stop it!" Michiko whispered. "Kokkuri-san will be offended and might do something bad. She's taken the trouble to show up, so give her some time."

Kate's face paled, and she nodded. Sweat trickled down her temple before she could wipe it with her free hand.

It grew even colder as they waited, and Michiko wished she'd put on a sweater before they'd started. Until the spirit left, none of them could move their fingers from the coin— or it might not leave. She'd heard of terrible things that had happened when a spirit lingered. Sophia, in her PJs, shivered too. Only Kate, still dressed in her hoodie and jeans, looked warm.

"Why won't it answer us?" said Sophia. "I don't like this at all."

"Patience," said Michiko. "Sometimes the spirit needs time to look around and think before it's ready to answer questions."

"I don't want it poking through my things!" said Kate in a fierce whisper, her eyes darting around. "Maybe you should ask all the questions, Michiko."

All at once a stink of rotting seaweed filled the room, making the three wrinkle their noses. The faintest of shadows hovered over the board, slowly taking shape. The girls watched with rapt attention as the ghostly wisps came together in the life-sized apparition of what looked like an old woman in a kimono, a dress that many Japanese women still wore.

Michiko stared at her, awed. She'd done it! She'd summoned her first spirit and she could not wait to tell her cousins about it, especially Hiro, whom she was very close to. Sophia and Kate seemed mesmerized too.

A sudden crash of thunder reverberated outside, making the girls jump. Michiko glanced at their fingers, still touching the coin, before looking up at the square of window illuminated by an arc of lightning. It had been a clear night; in fact, the next three days were supposed to be dry, per the LA weather report. *There had been no showers predicted this weekend, so why the thunder and lightning?* Though she found it odd, she focused on the game and her friends, who were getting nervous and impatient again.

"Sophia, you try," said Michiko.

"Which school did Lucas go to before he came here?" asked Sophia, tilting her head back to see the faintest of apparitions floating above her head. "Please tell us, K-san."

Michiko nodded approvingly as they all stared at the coin, still resting on the word YES.

The coin spun on the spot and was still. Somehow, the room seemed darker than before. There was a flash of heat on Michiko's face, as if she'd stepped too close to a bonfire, and then it was cold again. *What was going on?*

Sophia sat back with a huff. "This is rubbish. It's not working."

Michiko glared at her friend. How many times did she have to tell them both to be respectful? If they treated the spirit like a joke, she *wouldn't* answer them. Michiko had to take matters into her own hands. She had to ask the question that had been burning holes in her mind for months now.

"Kokkuri-san, what's wrong with Mom?" said Michiko. "Is she going to die?"

Silence. Her friends stared at her for what seemed like ages.

Kate was the first to recover. "What's wrong with your mom?"

"Why didn't you tell us?" said Sophia, looking hurt.

"I'm not sure," said Michiko, shrugging, trying to keep her voice steady. "She's had a hacking cough for months now and it won't get better. She's not eating or sleeping well, and the doctors can't figure out what's wrong with her. I'm sorry I didn't tell you both before. I . . . I just couldn't. It's why I've not invited you over to my place for a while." She kept her eyes lowered so they wouldn't see the tears welling up.

Wordlessly, Sophia and Kate both reached out a free hand and squeezed Michiko's shoulders. For a minute they were as one, sharing the pain she was feeling.

Around them the air seemed to get colder still, thicker even. The spirit was definitely in the room, watching them. Michiko felt her presence, but was she friendly or evil? Rain started drumming on the roof, drowning out all other sounds. If only Michiko could shut the window, it might be slightly warmer in the room. Too late for that now. The spirit was here, and until coin moved to YES when Michiko asked her to leave, neither could they.

After a reassuring nod from her friends, Michiko repeated her question. "Please, Kokkuri-san, tell me about my mom. Will she die?"

The coin jerked suddenly, and Michiko's breath caught in her throat. The coin inched across the board with agonizing slowness, making her lightheaded with panic as she imagined her father and her left to pick up the pieces of a life without Mom.

The coin came to rest on the word NO.

Michiko squeezed her eyes shut, relief flooding her. Someone pressed down hard on her finger. Michiko's eyes snapped open, and she realized her finger had almost slipped off the coin. Kate was keeping it in place.

"Thanks," Michiko whispered with a smile. It felt as if she'd just slid out from under an enormous boulder that had been sitting on her chest for months.

Sophia and Kate were both grinning too.

"Yay!" Sophia whooped.

"What she said," echoed Kate.

"Looks like she's finally answering questions," added Michiko. "Want to try again, Sophia?"

"Yes, please! Do we have algebra or ratios on next week's test, K-san?"

The spirit suddenly seemed to be a lot more chatty. Swiftly and sharply, the coin moved through the alphabet, spelling out A-L-G-E-B-R-A.

Kate and Sophia high-fived each other. Michiko couldn't help but let out a laugh. *This* was how it had been with her cousins. How it was supposed to go. She'd turned them from skeptics to believers! It felt thrilling to share this experience with her best friends.

"Umm, she didn't answer my question," said Kate.

"Go ahead," said Michiko casually. Now that the question of life and death had been answered, she was almost keen to know whom Lucas fancied.

"Whom does Lucas like, K-san?" asked Kate. "Which one of us gets to call him— boyfriend?" She giggled, her green eyes twinkling.

The coin did not move.

"Is Sadia a fave of Lucas's?" asked Sophia, pretending to gag.

No response.

"Kokkuri-san, please answer this last question and then you may leave us," said Michiko. "Whom does Lucas like best: Kate, Sophia, or someone else?"

At this, the coin zipped all over the board. It started spelling one word, faster than the ones from before, over and over again.

D-A-N-G-E-R

6

Michiko felt as if someone had pushed her into a tub of icy water. She stared at the coin, which now rested innocently on the letter R. Kate was as white as the walls, while Sophia's face twisted in anger. The ruckus of the surprise showers turned thunderstorm rang in their ears; the stench of rotting seaweed clogged their nostrils.

"Is this spirit messing with us?" snapped Sophia. "What danger? Is there a snake in the room?"

"We're all s-s-safe inside . . . aren't we?" Kate squeaked, her eyes darting around the room. "Oh, quit it, K-san!"

"Shhhh," said Michiko, looking around fearfully. "Please don't be disrespectful. If she gets angry . . ." Her voice trailed away as she peered at the shadowy corners of the room. *Why hadn't they left all the lights on? What danger was she talking about? Was Lucas in danger?* He very well might be, running around outside this time of night. Panicked thoughts darted around in her head like koi fish in a pond.

For what seemed like an eternity, the coin seemed to be stuck on the letter R. Michiko's arm started aching and threatened to give way. She wanted to end this *now*. The spirit sounded strange, or angry, or both. All she knew was this wasn't how it was supposed to go. At least they had answers to two questions. *And Mom will live*, she reminded herself. That alone was worth the trouble of convincing her friends to call Kokkuri-san using the Ouija board.

"I don't like this at all," said Kate. "Please tell her to go back, Michiko."

"I don't think she wants to answer the question about Lucas," said Michiko. "Sophia, do you agree we should send her back?"

Sophia nodded vigorously.

"Kokkuri-san, thank you for your time and your wisdom," said Michiko. "Please go back now." Her voice came out unnaturally high-pitched. She cleared her throat and tried again. "Kokkuri-san, please go back now. Thank you."

But the coin didn't budge. Around them, the air started thickening again, becoming heavier by the second. Michiko felt as if something were pressing down on her, trying to crush her alive. The thunderstorm grew more violent. A few drops spattered onto the floor through the open window, bringing the smell of fresh earth. Oh, how Michiko wanted to race to the window and gulp in a lungful of the clean air! But she couldn't. None of them could raise their fingers from the coin. Not until it moved back to the torii gate after passing YES to show that the spirit was leaving. She'd heard the warning repeatedly from her cousins over countless vacations in Japan.

Michiko took a deep breath, steadied her voice, and repeated the request again and again. There was no movement on the board.

Kate and Sophia looked terrified. Michiko dared not show how frightened *she* was, or they would have a complete meltdown. Especially poor Kate, who already appeared ready to faint. *I have to end this*, she told herself. She had suggested this game and forced the others to play. It was up to her to get them out.

"Kokkuri-san, is there something you want us to do before you leave?" asked Michiko, changing tactics. "We will help you if you tell us how." The idea had just occurred to her. Maybe the spirit was still lingering because she needed something from them?

The coin shifted slightly, and her heart lifted. Kate and Sophia leaned forward too, watching it eagerly. At last, this game would end! She couldn't wait to spend the coin and tear up the "board" into forty-eight pieces and scatter them. These were the rules of wrapping up every Ouija board session. Michiko even promised herself never to play this game again as she tried not to wrinkle her nose. The stink of seaweed mixed with something bitter had intensified in the time the coin had taken to slither across the board.

Fools.

Someone uttered it so softly, Michiko might have imagined it. Kate's and Sophia's eyes were glued to the coin, which was circling the board lazily, taking its time. This spirit was a trickster and a tormenter, Michiko could tell.

It finally slowed and moved to N. Then O. N-O.

"This is all *your* fault!" Kate burst out, tears spilling from her eyes. "I didn't want to do this, and you forced me, saying this was just some cute animal spirit. This seems like a mean spirit. She warned us of danger and now won't leave. Are we in danger from *her*?"

"What she said," Sophia added stiffly. "We have to be up early tomorrow. Tell the spirit to go, Michiko. If anyone can do it, *you* can." Her gaze swept the room.

"Kokkuri-san, will you please leave?" Michiko said in a trembling voice.

Suddenly she couldn't face Kate or Sophia. Why did she have to lie to her friends about doing this before? Clearly, she'd missed a step. And why couldn't she have just confided in them about Mom before dragging them into this mess? They were right—now they were in deep trouble all thanks to *her*. Michiko felt guilty and helpless.

Still the coin didn't move. Time crawled by, and they were all so tired and achy, they sagged against each other. No one spoke. Each time someone's finger slipped off the coin, one of the others would grab it in time. The air in the room turned fouler. The rain became a trickle, then finally stopped. At one point, the spirit sang a song in Japanese, which Michiko did not understand. It seemed to be in a dialect Michiko was not familiar with. What was the spirit trying to say by lingering here?

Michiko repeated her request over and over, her voice getting shriller. More time passed and when she finally glanced at her watch, it was *one* in the morning. They'd sat at the board for hours and the coin hadn't budged.

At two in the morning, a boom reverberated across the sky and lightning illuminated the landscape briefly. The power went out, extinguishing the lone lamp. None of the girls had a flashlight, nor could they have gotten up to get it.

They were trapped by the Ouija board and a spirit who refused to leave.

7

Michiko awoke with a start to the sound of pounding on the door. Sunlight was streaming in through the open window.

She looked at the board, and an icy hand squeezed her heart. They'd all fallen asleep on the floor and their fingers were off the coin, which still rested on NO.

Michiko sniffed the air. The room smelled of wet earth and sunshine. There wasn't the faintest whiff of seaweed. Had the spirit gotten tired and left? A chill lingered, but it could be the morning desert air and the fact that she was wearing only a T-shirt and jeans. The pounding continued, and Michiko jumped up.

"Michiko! Sophia! Kate!" Ms. Fraser called out. "You've missed breakfast and we're leaving for the dunes in twenty minutes. *What* are you girls up to? This is highly irresponsible. You should have been in the cafeteria half an hour ago!"

"Sorry, Ms. Fraser," Michiko called from behind the door. "My alarm didn't go off. We'll be out in a few minutes."

Ms. Fraser's footsteps receded among the excited chatter of students heading to their rooms after breakfast or making their way out for the day's excursions. When she turned around, she found Sophia and Kate staring at her as one, the events of the night clearly flooding back to mind. They'd just woken up and, after one look at the board, were clinging to each other, horrified.

"She hasn't left, has she?" asked Sophia. She sounded tired and furious.

Kate shook her head, looking at Michiko as if she were a pile of trash. "If you hadn't insisted that we play this dangerous game, we wouldn't be up half the night asking a spirit to leave! Now who knows where she is and if we're stuck with her forever?" She glanced around the room nervously. "If something bad happens to us, it'll be your fault. Yours *and* that spirit's."

"Guys, I think she's gone," said Michiko, though, in her heart, she knew this too was a lie. She'd put her best friends and herself in danger; now she'd have to figure it out on her own without scaring them further. She couldn't ruin the rest of the class trip for Kate and Sophia by admitting her worst suspicion. That if the spirit had left, the coin was bound to be resting at the torii gate after moving through YES. That Kokkuri-san was still here. "I'm so sorry for putting you both through this, but if she hasn't, I'll fix it. You have my word."

Kate stared hard at her, almost as if she could see into her heart— read her mind. She had always been the more perceptive of the two. "You mean that?"

Michiko nodded and placed an arm around each of her friends, hugging them close. "I promise."

But neither Kate nor Sophia returned the hug.

"Let's hurry," said Sophia. "If we're late, Ms. Fraser will be angrier than the spirit."

They made it to the lobby within fifteen minutes, where Lucas came up to them with three small brown paper bags.

"Breakfast," he said, and they each took one.

"That's so sweet, thanks, Lucas!" Kate gushed, her cheeks turning pink.

His voice dropped to a whisper. "The lights in your room were on late last night. You girls having a party or something?"

Michiko stared at Lucas, wondering how his late night out with Sasha had fared. A chill crept up the back of her neck, and she looked around but saw nothing out of the ordinary. "Or something," she said, devouring her butter croissant with gratitude. "Thanks for the breakfast. I'm starving."

While waiting her turn to use the bathroom earlier that morning, she'd managed to text the family group chat. Mom was out of bed and eating a light breakfast, a task that had been too demanding for her lately. Michiko took that as a sign that things at home would be better from now on. Relief warred with guilt as she glanced at Kate's and Sophia's faces.

"We were playing a childish game that Michiko suggested," said Sophia, glaring at her. "It was a bad idea, and we lost track of the time."

Michiko felt a stab in her heart. Sophia had never been *this* mean before, telling an outsider about their shenanigans.

"What game?" asked Lucas, his blue eyes sweeping over their heads and toward the entrance with a strange intensity, almost anger. But it was only Ms. Fraser striding out with their guide, Casey.

"Something I used to play back in Japan," said Michiko, flashing a warning look at Sophia and Kate. "Wouldn't interest you."

As Lucas walked away, Sophia looked at Kate, who held her gaze. There seemed to be an unspoken agreement between them as they turned back to Michiko with unfriendly eyes. They hadn't said a word to her while they'd dressed that morning and hurried out of the room. Even now, they whispered among themselves, but whenever she tried to join in, they clammed up and moved away. They were punishing her for last night and, truth be told, she couldn't blame them. She would have been angry too if her friends made her do something uncomfortable that they couldn't undo. In that moment, Michiko knew things were going downhill with their friendship, unless she fixed this. *Fast!*

"I'm sorry," she whispered, trailing behind them. "This wasn't supposed to happen. It's a game many kids play. I've played it several times, and the spirit has *always* gone back. Something is off this time—you have to believe it's not my fault!"

Her friends looked at her as if she were speaking a foreign language. It occurred to her then that they'd never had a serious fight about *anything* before. Even if one of them was mad, they would rally together and resolve the issue before it got too bad. This was the first time it was two against one.

After a while, she gave up trying to talk to them, focusing instead on the fact that Mom was going to be okay. *Besides, wasn't it possible that K-san (the short form was so much easier!) had already departed and simply forgotten to move the coin? Spirits can be forgetful, right?* she asked herself desperately.

"Listen up!" Casey's voice cut through the chatter. Everyone fell silent and gathered around her. "Today we'll be visiting the Kelso sand dunes, which is about a two-hour hike for the round trip from the trailhead. On the way, I'll point out the flora and fauna of the fascinating Mojave

Desert. You'll be amazed at how animals have adapted to the harsh conditions. Once we're on foot, always look before you step. I repeat, the Mojave green rattlesnake is one of the *deadliest* ones in the area. Though the snakes will head for shade as the day grows warmer, we still need to be careful. If you hear a rattling sound, freeze!" She took out her phone, tapped a few keys, and held it out toward them. "This is what it sounds like."

A frenzied sound filled the air. Like that of an angry child with a rattle, demanding attention. Casey played it a couple more times, moving around the group of students so everyone could hear it clearly.

"We'll take a short detour before we head for the buses. Ready?"

There was a chorus of yeses.

"Follow me!" Casey said and started walking.

Michiko sighed as she trailed behind the rest of the students. Kate and Sophia, who were studiously ignoring her, were way up front.

"Are *you* still here, K-san? Give me a sign if you are," she said under her breath.

Yet another chill brushed the back of her neck, making Michiko whip around—only to see the flag outside the lodge suddenly unfurling with gusto. All without a hint of a breeze.

8

Michiko hurried to catch up with the others. No one had noticed the flag, but she couldn't help taking one more look. When she turned around, she came face to face with Ms. Fraser.

"Michiko, is something wrong?" Ms. Fraser said, frowning. "It's most unlike you to be so inattentive."

Michiko shook her head, aware of nineteen pairs of eyes on her. She wished she could turn invisible. Now everyone would think she was a weirdo, and she didn't even have the support of her friends. "All good, Ms. Fraser. Couldn't fall asleep last night. Strange bed and all."

"Hmm," said Ms. Fraser. "Keep up. You can get to bed a little earlier tonight, if you wish."

When Michiko nodded, Ms. Fraser swiveled on her heel and headed back to the front of the group, leaving Michiko to follow. Though she tried to play it cool, she couldn't shake the feeling that someone was following her. As she passed under a tree, a sudden chill and the stench of rotting seaweed—so strong that she wanted to gag—wafted around her. Something cold slipped down her neck.

The Mojave green. *I'm going to die!*

"Snake!" she screamed. "It's wriggling down my back!"

Casey came charging up to her as she squirmed, trying to get hold of whatever was slithering down her neck, bracing for the deadly bite, for the poison to start coursing through her veins. She was so scared; she could barely breathe.

"What is it, Michiko?" asked Casey. "Stand still and let me look."

"I hope neither of us get bitten," Michiko managed to gasp, her heart galloping in her chest. *This* must have been the danger K-san was talking about.

All eyes were on her as Casey reached into the back of her hoodie and drew out a long piece of spongy cactus, cold with the rain.

"Nothing to worry about," said Casey cheerfully, deflating Michiko's panic. "This must be due to the rainstorm last night. Sometimes water saturates the cacti and makes a weak bit fall off."

Michiko caught sight of Kate and Sophia staring at her white-faced. But neither of them came close, to talk to her or reassure her. That hurt more than any snakebite could have.

Michiko decided she had to put K-san out of her head and focus on the trip. If not, she'd be jumping at shadows all the time. She forced herself to listen to Casey, who was now at the front of the group.

"If you keep very silent, you might see some of the wildlife," said Casey. "They're as curious about you as you are about them."

The desert was quiet, and the smell of damp earth was fast dissipating as the day grew warmer. Casey stopped beside a gigantic Joshua tree. It had a shaggy trunk that ended in branches, each topped with a fuzz of pointed green leaves. It looked like a giant cheerleader in the desert, waving its green pom-poms. A few clicked pictures with their phones. Lucas and Sasha tried climbing it before Casey told them to cut it out. A jackrabbit peeped out from behind a rock, its large ears almost translucent. Just then, a piercing scream shattered the flurry of clicks.

"SNAKE!"

Panic rippled through the crowd again as they raced away from the student who'd screamed.

It was Kate.

She stood rooted to the spot, with her trembling hand pointing at something on the ground. It was moving fast, zigzagging across the sandy desert floor, heading for a clump of creosote bushes.

Casey reached Kate in the blink of an eye, putting an arm around her shaking shoulders. "Well-spotted—but that was a harmless grass snake, also green. You remember I told you about the rattling sound?"

Kate's shoulders relaxed, though her face was still white. From afar, Michiko saw that dark circles ringed her eyes and she looked exhausted. Once again, she felt overcome with horrible guilt for forcing her friends to take part in the game. Lack of sleep and paranoia were to blame for her jumpiness, Michiko figured. Sophia, looking equally tired, approached to comfort Kate. Neither seemed to mind nor care that Michiko wasn't in their huddle.

In trying to save her mother, had she lost her best friends?

"The rattling sound comes from the tip of the tail, which vibrates," Casey was still talking to Kate as the class scattered. "It's their way of warning off predators—a defense mechanism. This one didn't have it, right?"

Kate gave Casey a watery smile. "I'm deathly afraid of snakes."

"So am I," said Casey, winking. "The most important thing to remember is that they're as afraid of you as you are of them. They'd rather avoid confrontation if they can. If you're careful and respect their space, they'll slither away." She paused before calling out, "Remember, all: snakes attack only when they're threatened or disturbed. Look where you're going and if you see one, freeze! It will move away from you, and no harm done."

"That's excellent advice," added Ms. Fraser.

Finally, they got to the bus that was to take them to the dunes, a twenty-minute drive from the visitor center. When they got out, a searing heat swept over them. In the distance, the dunes were majestic and glinting golden in the late morning sun. The road leading up to the dunes was relatively flat. As they hiked, Casey stopped along the way to point out a flower or the tracks made by various desert fauna.

Closer to the dunes, the sand grew softer under their feet, making it harder to walk on. Casey reminded them to refresh their sunscreen and hydrate. A few students who were not used to walks and hikes were starting to slow down. Michiko was enjoying it thoroughly. The only thing that marred her enjoyment was the fact that Kate and Sophia were not by her side.

At the foot of the dunes, Casey stopped. "Listen up everyone. Yesterday you heard the dunes sing. Today we'll find out *how*, and make them sing again. Ready?"

There were half-hearted yeses from those who were already exhausted, but Sadia seemed into it and Karim was naturally the most enthusiastic. Michiko was almost looking forward to the magic of the dunes too, despite the heat that was pricking the exposed skin on her arms and the occasional whiffs of rotting seaweed that apparently only she could smell. She wondered if Kate and Sophia felt K-san's presence too. But she stopped herself from going down that rabbit hole.

Casey smiled. "Trust me, this climb will be worth it. Get to the ridge, space yourselves out, and wait for my instructions. Also, the first one up gets a Mojave National Preserve T-shirt and thermos. They're great gifts."

Everyone took off as if running from a fire. Sophia and Kate started racing up too, holding hands. Lucas and Sasha were right behind them. Sophia turned around and said something to Lucas. They all laughed. None of them even glanced toward Michiko, who, feeling like a pariah, tried to ignore the dull ache spreading through her. It was a punch to the gut to see her best friends leaving her behind for cooler company.

As she looked ahead, suddenly her skin seemed to be on fire and the golden dunes turned black. Michiko blinked . . . and the dunes looked normal again. She fished out the sunscreen from her pocket and slathered some onto her face and arms. *Must be the sun*, she thought to herself as she started hurrying up the slope.

"Come on, Michiko," said Casey. "You aren't scared of heights, are you? These are barely anything and the view from the top is fantastic."

Michiko smiled and shook her head. "I've hiked mountains higher than this."

Casey gave her a thumbs up and hurried on, keeping an eye on all the students and their teacher laboring up the slope.

Hauling herself up, Michiko decided there was nothing to do but enjoy the dunes. After all, she couldn't undo last night. And if Kate and Sophia gave up on her and found new friends, maybe she could too. She already had a spirit "friend" who was stuck to her.

9

The sun climbed higher in the sky and mist rose from the ground, evaporating rapidly. Michiko clambered up the sandy slope. It was hard work and her T-shirt stuck to her back with sweat. For every step she took, she slid back two. Almost all the students were facing the same problem. Only Casey was almost to the top, moving sideways and treading lightly.

Ms. Fraser, behind Michiko, was muttering to herself, "You can do this, Minnie, come on, up you go. That's the spirit."

Michiko almost laughed out loud, when her eyes strayed to Kate and Sophia and her classmates, who were almost up to the top. Her mouth tightening to a thin line, she immediately picked up her pace. *Once we get back and K-san is gone, everything will be back to normal*, Michiko told herself. It *had* to be. Michiko couldn't believe they would continue to shut her out forever. *Would they?* Michiko glanced around her. She was surrounded by chattering, squealing company, yet she'd never felt so alone in her life.

"Did you have a fight with Sophia and Kate?" came an

intrusive question. It was Sadia, who'd slowed down, waiting for Michiko to catch up to her. "Why are they ignoring you?"

The questions were stabs to her heart. "Mind your own business," said Michiko.

Sadia reddened, and Michiko instantly regretted her unprompted meanness. Sadia had never sought her out before today, even when Michiko had tried to be friendly. Sadia's innate confidence was a constant reminder that she wasn't, which irritated her even more. But why was Sadia being nice to her all of a sudden?

"There's no need to be rude," said Sadia. "You looked sad, and I was only trying to help."

"Sorry—" Michiko started to say, but Sadia had already sped up and was out of hearing range before she could finish.

Michiko was the last one to reach the top but, as Casey had rightly said, the view was worth it. Staring out at the panoramic view, her heart felt lighter. The desert ground, shimmering in the heat, looked like an alien landscape with bobble-headed Joshua trees breaking up the monotony. Against a perfectly blue horizon, in the distance, was a collection of large boulders pockmarked with holes. A breath of wind flitted by and cooled her sweating face. It smelled faintly of wet earth, which she knew now—thanks to Casey— was the smell of the creosote bushes that dotted the desert floor. If only she could have shared this experience with her two best friends.

Following instructions from Casey, they all stood, evenly spaced, along the ridge of the massive dune, which undulated like a gigantic snake in both directions.

"Watch me," said Casey.

She straddled the ridge and pushed the sand down with her boot. At first, nothing happened.

"Don't think the sand is in the mood to sing this morning," said Lucas. Someone giggled.

"Give it a few seconds," said Casey, and pushed some more sand down, which started trickling downhill, gathering momentum. As it raced down, an eerie wail emanated from it. The same as the night before.

Despite the heat, a chill gripped Michiko. For one, the stench of seaweed was strong. And overlying that was the fact that her body seemed to be on fire again. What was going on? To her, the dunes sounded too ghostly for comfort. But now that everyone knew what to do, they were all pushing down the sand. As a result, plaintive wailing and buzzing reverberated through the stillness of the desert. As if a hundred spirits were crying in unison.

"HELP!" a student yelled.

Michiko recognized the voice and raced toward it, the sand sucking at her feet so that it felt like she were racing through tar. But she *had* to get to her friend, so she ran as hard and fast as she could.

Sophia had broken through the line of students along the ridge and was tumbling head over heels down the steep slope. It was as if she'd lost her balance and could do nothing to break the fall. Lucas, who'd tried to grab her, stood with his arm outstretched. Except for Kate's sobbing, the desert was suddenly quiet. The wailing had died down now that all the students were frozen, watching Sophia hurtle to the ground like a rag doll, screaming all the way down.

Casey was racing after her, keeping her balance and staying upright. After what felt like an hour but must have been no more than a few seconds, Sophia finally flopped

POSSESSED

onto the desert floor and lay still, her screams stopping abruptly. In an instant, Casey was beside Sophia. Ms. Fraser was next to arrive.

Atop the dune, Michiko had reached Kate and was wrapping her arms around her sobbing friend. "What happened?" she asked. "How did she fall?"

"I don't know," Kate said, turning a tear-blotched face toward Michiko. "One minute we were making the sands sing and the next minute she toppled forward and kept going."

"Come on," said Michiko, her heart slamming against her ribs so hard, she thought they'd crack. "She'll need us."

They raced down the slope toward a disheveled Sophia, who was now sitting up with a dazed look, while Casey prodded her ankles, hands, and neck. She spoke to Sophia softly, telling her to look this way and that and asking questions.

"Anything broken?" asked Michiko, staring at Sophia, her heart pounding.

Sophia shook her head as tears streamed down her face, streaking her dusty cheeks.

"Thank God you're okay," squeaked Kate as she clung to Sophia. "One minute you were beside me and then you were halfway down."

"Give her some space, please," said Casey. She stood up and spoke to the lodge on her walkie-talkie, asking for the jeep so Sophia could be driven back to the Kelso Depot. No cars were allowed on the trail leading up to the dunes, but it seemed they made exceptions for accidents. As soon as she finished, she knelt beside Sophia, watching her with concern.

In the meantime, by unspoken agreement, Ms. Fraser gathered the other students and led them some distance away. She must have told them to wait there because she came back alone.

"Talk to us," said Michiko, close to tears on seeing Sophia's warm, brown face pale and scared.

"I'm fine," said Sophia, not meeting their eyes. Particles of shimmering sand stuck to her skin.

"What *happened*?" Michiko asked again. "Did you lose your balance?"

Sophia's eyes narrowed as she looked past them to the top of the dune, towering over them.

Casey and Ms. Fraser leaned closer, the guide adding, "Please tell us why you fell. This may be a safety issue and we must address it immediately before we let anyone climb the dunes again."

"I-I tripped over my shoelace," said Sophia in a flat voice. "That was all."

Casey watched Sophia for a long minute, saying nothing. Her friend refused to meet her eye and Michiko was certain there was more to the story. Her instinct told her K-san was involved. After all, hadn't she warned them of danger? And hadn't Michiko smelled the seaweed, which she now came to associate with K-san's presence?

"The main thing is you're safe and nothing's broken," said Casey at long last. "Let's get you back to the lodge, where you can rest." Her walkie-talkie crackled, and she walked away to answer it. When she returned, Casey and Ms. Fraser had a whispered conversation a short distance away from the girls.

Michiko crouched beside Sophia and stared into her friend's pale face. "What really happened? You didn't trip, did you?"

"What makes you say that?" said Sophia, flashing her

friend a glare. Her voice shook, and her eyes kept flicking to the top of the dune, to the ridgeline.

A deathly chill permeated Michiko despite the scorching heat. Sophia was always cool in a crisis, and it took a *lot* to scare her or shut her up. *What had happened up there?*

"I tripped over my shoelace," said Sophia again. "How many times do I have to repeat that?"

She was lying, but Michiko said nothing as her eyes swept over Sophia's slip-on footwear.

"Listen up everyone," said Casey. "We're all heading back to the Kelso Depot. We'll do some activities closer to home so Sophia can head to her room and get some rest."

The ride back was subdued as Casey shared the science behind the singing dunes. It was a combination of the steep slopes, the dry weather, and the winds, which caused the sounds. Only a few students were paying attention. Some were tired and others kept glancing at Sophia. It was hard to have a conversation with so many people around, but Michiko promised herself that as soon as the three were alone, she'd get to the bottom of this.

Once Sophia went off with the staff, the rest explored the Kelso Depot with Casey as their knowledgeable guide. The first depot had been opened in 1905 to provide services to passengers and railroad employees. It also served as a stop for water for the steam locomotives. It was then renovated, becoming the Kelso Depot Visitor Center in 2005. They watched a twenty-minute orientation film in the theater and then Casey allowed them to explore the dormitories, the baggage room, and the ticket office. It was fascinating to see how people lived in the first half of the twentieth century. Next up was the Kelso City Jail, which were two rusted metal cages.

Everyone had fun getting in there to take pictures. Lucas and Sasha goofed around, sticking their hands out of the bars and pleading for help while their classmates clicked photos.

It would have been a fun afternoon excursion wandering through this Spanish Mission Revival style building if Michiko hadn't been worried sick about Sophia and the thought of returning to their room. Would they have to spend another night with K-san lingering there?

Kate must have felt the same way because she had barely said a word to Michiko, even though Michiko was trailing her the whole way and trying hard to get her to talk.

"I hope Sophia is okay," Lucas asked, falling into step beside them. "That was an epic roll." His eyes were a darker blue than usual, almost black. *Could a person's eyes change color all that much?* Michiko wondered.

"She'll be fine," said Kate, her tone brusque.

"Do you mind giving us some space?" said Michiko to Lucas, trying not to snap. She needed to chat with Kate in private.

Lucas nodded. "Catch you guys later." He sauntered away.

"There's something you're not telling me about what happened," said Michiko when everyone else was out of earshot. "I want the truth."

Kate whipped around. "Just before Sophia fell, there was a random icy draft, just like last night. I remember because Lucas noticed it, too." She paused and gave Michiko a venomous look. "I think it was that spirit of yours who made Sophia fall. I think the danger she was warning us about was *her*. She's trying to kill us. There's your truth."

10

The blood drained from Michiko's face. She was lightheaded and had the desperate urge to throw up. But she took a deep breath, trying to calm down. No way was she going to barf in front of an audience. She forced herself to focus on what Kate was telling her.

"K-san couldn't have done this," said Michiko. "She's a trickster, not a killer!"

"How do you know for sure, and how do I know you're not lying again?" asked Kate, her green eyes blazing. "You've put us all in danger because you wanted to find out about your mother. You were sneaky, and you used us—just admit it." Kate spat out the last few words.

It felt as if her friend had hurled a handful of glass at her and the shards had lodged right in her heart. The added fact that she'd still not disclosed a minor but significant element to her friends—that she'd never done this before—made Michiko drown in a sea of guilt. But could there be a grain of truth to Kate's accusations? Was K-san, the trickster spirit, warning them of danger and then harming them too? If only K-san had been specific about the danger, it would have been more helpful than just spelling out "danger."

"You two," said Casey from the front, where she was pointing out even more of the natural beauty of the desert. "Enough of the chatter. Pay attention."

"Sorry," said Kate. She moved toward Lucas and Sasha and stayed as far away from Michiko as possible for the remainder of the walk around the depot.

The staff had organized a small picnic in a section of the depot that was closed to the public. Everyone helped themselves to juice and an assortment of wraps and sandwiches. Michiko wasn't hungry but she forced herself to eat something as she watched Kate, still subdued but chatting with Lucas and Sasha. For a brief second the scene dimmed as she ate by herself, and the color seemed to leach out from the world around her. When she blinked, it was back to normal. Michiko tried to shake off the feeling of impending doom and act natural. She was in over her head, and it was a terrifying thought that she had dragged her two best friends into this mess.

When they finally got back to the lodge at almost five in the evening, Michiko was exhausted. The sun was starting to set, turning the sky a fiery red, but she barely noticed it. Instead, she thought about how much she would have enjoyed exploring the depot with Kate and Sophia. History was a passion of hers, which was one of the reasons she'd signed up for this trip. But she couldn't enjoy *any* of it. She could only think of getting back to check on Sophia and see if K-san was still haunting their room—or worse, causing all this unexplained trouble. The image of the coin resting on the letter R, the last letter in D-A-N-G-E-R, made her throat dryer than the desert air.

POSSESSED

"Freshen up, everyone, and gather in the cafeteria," said Ms. Fraser as soon as everyone in the group had assembled in the lobby. "We'll have an early dinner and discuss what we've seen and learned. Casey will answer any questions you have. After that, you have some free time before a stargazing session, then it's lights out."

Michiko was about to race off when Ms. Fraser called out to her, "Michiko, wait up. I'll come with you. I want to see how Sophia is doing. If she's better, she can join us for dinner."

She would have preferred to go alone, but Michiko couldn't disobey her teacher. Michiko forced herself to walk slowly beside Ms. Fraser, who chattered on about the exciting day and everything they'd encountered.

"What did you think of the Kelso Depot and all that we've seen so far?" Ms. Fraser asked.

"It's been great!" said Michiko, trying to sound enthusiastic.

KATE WAS ALREADY in their room, talking to Sophia in a low voice. They stopped as soon as she and Ms. Fraser entered the room and stared at her coolly. Her best friends were not only treating her like a stranger but now making no effort to conceal their annoyance at Michiko. She glanced around the room and took a deep sniff. No smell and no sign of K-san.

"How are you, my dear?" said Ms. Fraser, coming up to Sophia. "That was quite a tumble you took. Thank goodness it was sand and not gravel. I don't know what I would have told your parents. As it is, I'll be reporting this incident and I'm so glad that you're unhurt."

Sophia smiled, but Michiko knew it wasn't real. Her eyes were cold and hard when she glanced at Michiko. "I'm fine. It was nothing at all, Ms. Fraser, except clumsiness. My bad."

"Will you join us for dinner, or would you prefer to eat in your room?" Ms. Fraser asked. "Casey is also going to show us some more pictures from when Kelso was a working depot. I'm sure you'll find it interesting."

"I'd love to, Ms. Fraser," said Sophia. "I'll be right there."

"Would you like me to wait—," Ms. Fraser started to say but Kate piped up.

"I'll help her," said Kate.

"Me too," said Michiko. She was dying to ask Sophia if there had been any activity, any sign that the spirit was still lingering, but she kept her impatience reined in.

Ms. Fraser smiled. "I'm so glad to see you friends looking after each other. I miss my school friends. We used to have such a great time, but then we all grew up and went our separate ways. Cherish this time, my dears, for once gone, it never comes back." She left the room and an awkward silence ballooned as Michiko looked from Sophia to Kate.

"Are you guys never going to speak to me again?" Michiko asked. "I'm so very sorry. What more do you want me to say? I only wanted to ask about Mom because she's been so ill and I was afraid she would . . ." Michiko stopped, unable to finish. She swallowed and fell silent.

"There's no sign of K-san," said Sophia, thawing a little. "Maybe she got tired and left."

"So, what really happened?" asked Michiko. "Kate said she felt a chilly breeze and then you fell."

Sophia took a deep breath and hugged her knees to her chest. "I did not fall. Someone pushed me."

"What?" said Michiko, her heart thudding painfully. "Are you sure?"

POSSESSED

"You think I rolled down the dunes in front of the entire class, plus Lucas, for the fun of it?" snapped Sophia.

"Sorry," said Michiko, sitting on the bed and reaching out for Sophia's hand. Sophia jerked it away. Michiko took a deep breath and continued, "I'm not doubting that you fell. I'm surprised at the possibility of K-san pushing you. This makes no sense."

Kate wrung her hands, her eyes filling with tears. "None of this Ouija nonsense makes sense. We should *never* have agreed to play something this dangerous."

"You're right, Kate . . . but we can't turn back time," said Michiko, trying to be as patient as she could. "Why don't I think of a way to deal with this?" Her cousin Hiro was two years older than her and had played this game countless times. In fact, the first time Michiko had played was with him. She trusted him completely, and if anyone knew what to do, it was him. She had to get in touch with him right away.

But Kate and Sophia only looked at her with disgust, not softening in the slightest.

Michiko could lose her temper, too. She could remind them they had had questions, too, which they'd wanted answered. But that would mean going around in circles, blaming each other. If they couldn't come up with a solution, Hiro would. Japan was about sixteen hours ahead of the United States. It was nearing 6 p.m. in LA, which meant it would be almost 10 a.m. in Tokyo. She would call him as soon as they'd finished with dinner.

Just the thought of a solution made her feel calmer, grounded. She remembered the last time she'd played with Hiro. His voice was soft yet commanding and the spirit had come, answered questions, and then left. There had been no drama like the one she, Kate, and Sophia were facing.

"Let's go to the cafeteria or Ms. Fraser will come looking for us," said Michiko, getting to her feet when neither of them responded to her proposal. "I got us into this mess and, I *promise*, I will get us out of it."

11

The evening turned out to be fun, despite the worry that gnawed silently at Michiko. Since Kate and Sophia were ignoring her again, she texted Hiro discreetly and waited for a reply as she ate by herself.

Famished from their excursions, the group had readily dug into a buffet of sandwiches and assorted veggies with dip. There was also juice and iced tea, and an extensive selection of healthy baked foods for dessert. After a full day of roaming around in the scorching sun, the cold dinner was delicious, and they all had seconds and thirds. While they ate, Casey showed them black-and-white slides from the early 1900s, when the depot was still functional, and a steam-powered train pushed the coal carts up the hill. This was now renamed the Cima Dome.

"It's 1500 feet high," said Karim. "And I read that it's best viewed from a distance to appreciate its near perfect symmetry."

"Well done," said Casey. "Someone has done their homework."

There were groans from a few students. Some even

booed Karim, who looked down at his feet. *He's a geek who loves facts, so why can't they just leave him alone?* thought Michiko. *To each his own.*

"I'm freezing," Sadia said suddenly. "Why is it so cold in here when it's scorching outside?"

Michiko shivered, looking around warily for the source of the chill. *Was K-san back?*

Kate and Sophia exchanged glances and stared at her accusingly.

"That's on me," said Casey with a laugh. "With so many of us in the cafeteria, I turned up the air conditioning. Should I ask the staff to turn it down?"

"Yes, please," Sadia replied. There was a chorus of yeses.

Michiko slumped against her chair in relief. Her friends were right. This had been a *bad* idea. Instead of enjoying a fun weekend, she was constantly worrying about the spirit not leaving, plus the danger she'd warned them about. The more Michiko thought about it, the surer she became that she never should have taken the risk—even for a good reason, even for Mom.

Her only hope now was her cousin Hiro, whose response finally lit up her screen. Trying not to draw attention to herself, Michiko tucked her phone under the table and exchanged furtive texts with him.

M: Need your help urgently, Hiro. Played Kokkuri-san and don't know if she went away. Seems like she's still hanging around?? Plus she said something scary

H: WHAT??? You know this isn't something you take lightly. Tell me you're joking, Miko

M: Nope! We wanted to ask about a boy in class

H: BAD reason

M: And Mom. She's not well

H: What's wrong with her?

Michiko was expecting the inevitable question. Mom had insisted they not tell anyone back home about her condition or they'd worry about her, and rightly so. But before she could type out a reply, a shadow fell over her. Michiko looked up, and there was Ms. Fraser with her arm outstretched.

No!

"Even if we're not in a classroom, this is a learning opportunity," said Ms. Fraser. "I expect the same level of discipline and that means no phones or other distractions."

"I'm sorry, Ms. Fraser, it won't happen again," said Michiko, making no move to give the phone to her.

"I know, because your phone will be in *my* pocket," said Ms. Fraser. "I'm worried about you, Michiko. You and your roommates were late for the excursion and now you're not paying attention. If there's anything you'd like to share with me, we can step outside."

It was too small a room for anyone to have missed that exchange, even though Ms. Fraser spoke softly. All unsmiling eyes—including those of her best friends—were on Michiko, and her face felt warm. They'd all check their phones now and then, but none of the others had been caught. She'd been careless, and she was annoyed with herself. *Way to climb up the popularity chart*, she thought to herself dryly.

"I really need to keep my phone, Ms. Fraser," said Michiko in a low voice. "My mom is not well, and I might get a call..."

The teacher's expression softened immediately. "I understand that you're worried. But I'm sure she will be fine." She took a deep breath. "Don't forget, everyone's parents have the contact numbers for the school, the principal, the lodge, *and* my cell phone. If there's any kind of emergency, they know how to reach us. But I'm sure it will not come to that."

Except this was really about Hiro and how she was going to get K-san to leave. "Thank you, Ms. Fraser. Please let me keep the phone. I'll put it away and pay attention. You have my word."

"I'll let it go this once," said Ms. Fraser before walking away. "Class, this goes for all of you. No phones while we're learning."

Michiko saw Kate and Sophia rolling their eyes in her direction. Feeling sick at how unwanted she was in their company, she couldn't help but glance at her phone despite promising not to, where waiting messages from Hiro blinked for her attention.

H: Hello? Miko?

H: ????????

H: We need to talk. And BE CAREFUL. Stay calm but sound CONFIDENT. Spirits can sense weakness in your voice

H: If Kokkuri-san never really left, this could be VERY bad news

12

"Go wander, relax, and recharge," Ms. Fraser said after the slideshow. "We'll meet at the entrance around 7.45 to look at the constellations. It's going to be a cloudless night, and this far out of the city, we'll get a very clear view of the stars. Please don't be late."

Most fled to their respective rooms. Some made a beeline outside to get some fresh air.

Michiko wasn't keen to go back to the room and face Kate and Sophia, but she didn't want to talk to anyone else either. Hiro's last message had made her sick to her stomach. This trickster spirit was playing with their *minds*—by warning them of danger and then hurting them! *Had K-san somehow pushed Sophia? What if the accident had been fatal? What if Sophia had snapped her neck?* She shuddered at the thought of how horribly wrong this could have gone—and still could go.

Her head buzzing with questions, Michiko wandered out the main door. She glanced at the ground for any sign of movement, but there was none. It was dusk—the perfect time for snakes and other nocturnal creatures to be out and about. That Mojave green's toxicity was emblazoned in her mind and the last thing she wanted to do was step on one.

The heat in the air was slowly dissipating. The smell of the creosote bush—like wet earth—mingled with the smell of hot rock and dry vegetation. Michiko took in a deep breath. This place smelled so clean and different compared to the heart of the city, where the smells of petrol, food, sweat, and an occasional garbage truck filled the air.

Up ahead, Karim and Sadia were sharing binoculars. They'd spotted coyotes and were asking Casey for more information.

"They belong to the dog family called Canidae," Casey was saying. "They're small and lighter in color than those living in colder regions or other habitats. Although they're carnivores, these may also eat plants. This adaptability, as well as being able to forage for food in the day, has contributed to their survival. They have quite a distinctive ho—"

As if on cue, a coyote howled. Another answered. The dunes sang back. It sounded as if the night symphony had started.

But something was marring the beauty of the moment. Michiko sniffed hard at an offensive whiff in the air. Her sensitive nose was picking up a smell no one else seemed to have noticed. *Had some animal died? Or maybe the garbage bin behind the kitchen was open, and the food was stinking in this heat?* At least it didn't stink like seaweed, she thought to herself, following her nose around the side of the lodge.

At the far end of the lodge were some steps, on which sat a lone figure. She squinted in the dark to identify the silhouette. It was Lucas, and, for once, he was by himself.

Michiko strolled forward, then stopped. The horrible smell was coming from the sandwich he was chomping on!

Ugh! Couldn't he notice the stink? Whatever meat was in it had clearly spoiled.

"Stop!" she said, running up to him and knocking the last bit of sandwich from his hands.

Lucas jumped to his feet, startled. "Why did you do that?" he said, his blue eyes now so dark with anger, they looked midnight black.

This guy can sure be weird sometimes, thought Michiko, taking a hasty step back. "What's in that sandwich?" she asked.

"Baloney," said Lucas, gazing at the remnants lying in the dust. "I'd saved it from lunchtime because I wasn't hungry then ... and I don't like wasting food."

"Is that right?" said Michiko, wondering if that "lunchtime" had been a week ago. "It's obviously spoiled. Can't you smell it? It must taste gross."

Lucas shrugged. "Shoot! I had a bad cold last week. Can't taste or smell much." He took a deep sniff and shook his head. "Hey, thanks for stopping me. I might have been very sick."

"You could still get food poisoning, so watch out," said Michiko. "You'd finished eating most of it." The sun had dropped behind the dunes and suddenly the air turned chilly, as if someone had turned the air conditioner on outdoors. "Anyway, let's get back inside before we're missed. I don't want to run into anything out here in the dark."

"Sure," said Lucas, stooping to pick up the sandwich, which he carefully wrapped in a piece of parchment. "I'll throw this in the bin when we get inside. Mustn't leave food out here for the wild animals."

"Good thinking. In any case, we should report this to Casey," said Michiko as they started back to the entrance of the lodge. "If the cafeteria is serving food that spoils so quickly, we're all going to be sick. They need to be more careful and check expiry dates."

"You're sounding like Ms. Fraser!" snapped Lucas before composing himself. "I'll take care of it. I don't want to get anyone in trouble."

Michiko only nodded, keeping some distance between them. His breath still stank of spoiled meat, and it made her queasy. If Kate and Sophia could see, and smell their heart-throb now, she was sure they'd be over him in a hurry.

Back indoors, they parted ways and Michiko had no choice but to head back to the room. She knew her cousin would be in the middle of a school day by now, so she hammered out a terse reply.

Not sure about Mom. Lots of tests. No conclusive results, but K-san told me she's going to be fine. Just tell me how to send her back. Call me ASAP!!!

She stopped right outside their room, where she could hear the animated voices of Kate and Sophia. The second Michiko swung open the door, they fell silent.

"Were you talking about me?" asked Michiko, looking from one to the other.

Kate stared at the ground, wringing her hands. It was a dead giveaway. Sophia stared at Michiko. She'd always been the braver one.

"I think we should tell Ms. Fraser everything," said Sophia. "What we did, about the spirit, and that someone pushed me from the dunes. If there is an evil spirit from another world lurking around, we're all in danger."

"Listen to yourself, Sophia," said Michiko, her mouth suddenly dry. She had to stop Sophia from telling *anyone* about the Ouija board and K-san. It might anger the spirit even more, and then who knew what she'd do? "Do you think Ms. Fraser, or anyone else, will believe us? They'll

POSSESSED

think we're being silly, and we'll be the butt of all their jokes. Three weirdos who think their room is haunted. Is that what you want?"

"Michiko may be right," said Kate, who looked ill. "We shouldn't do anything rash."

Michiko knew Kate hated any sort of public ridicule and went out of her way to fit in. In fact, they all wanted to look cool, and this would have just the opposite effect.

"Whatever, I'm out of here," Sophia cut her off and strode to the door, her face screwed up in anger. "Looks like Michiko's totally wrong about how to send the spirit back, and now she's *attacked* me. You could be next." Locking eyes with Kate, she grabbed the door handle and pulled.

"It won't open," said Sophia, paling. She used both hands and pulled harder. The door didn't budge. She ran back to Kate, looking around. "She's here, isn't she?"

Within seconds, the room turned frigid and dense. In the deathly silence, a faint murmur emanated from the far corner. As if someone were praying or chanting, unseen.

"To the board," said Michiko. "Quick!"

13

It felt like a bad case of déjà vu. They crowded around the Ouija board again, their fingers on the coin. Michiko had hastily pulled on a sweater before they sat down. She was determined to sit up all night if that's what it took to get rid of this spirit. She would rest only when the spirit left.

Sophia and Kate sat on either side of her, but this time, instead of anticipation, there was fear, and anger, emanating from them both. If Michiko sent the spirit back, maybe their friendship would survive. Right now, it was doomed.

The muttering had stopped, but the air remained frigid. Michiko thought she felt K-san move around the room, eddies of icy drafts in her wake. Their breaths plumed in front of their faces and the foul smell of seaweed intensified.

"Kokkuri-san, please go back home now," said Michiko, trying to sound strong and in control, as Hiro had suggested. *He'd* always sounded like he was in charge when he'd played the Ouija board. In truth, Michiko had never felt so scared. All the more because there was one important fact she was still keeping from her best friends—like having led a summoning. Dread filled her at the thought of telling them

POSSESSED

the truth. And so, again, she decided against it. "Kokkuri-san, please go back home now," she repeated.

The coin did not move.

"Kokkuri-san, it is time for you to go," said Michiko. "We do not need your help. You *must* go." A trickle of sweat skated down her back. *What if K-san haunted them for the rest of their lives?* The thought was so unbearable, she whimpered. In hindsight, what she wouldn't do to go back in time and find another way to figure out what was wrong with Mom.

She replayed the scene from the night before in her mind but with a much better ending. She'd set up the board and had called Kate and Sophia to join her. They had both seemed reluctant. Kate had just found a Rom-com they all wanted to see, streaming on YouTube. Michiko had decided to abandon the Ouija board given that she'd never done it on her own before. She would find another way to get more information about Mom's illness—a more scientific way. They had watched the movie huddled in one bed, laughing through the evening, and had eventually gone to bed.

"Michiko! She's saying something!" hissed Kate. She elbowed Michiko hard with her free arm, jerking her out of her reverie.

Michiko snapped back to the horror of the present moment. They were still at the board. The room was freezing, and the renewed muttering was now coming from their bathroom.

"Shall we go look?" asked Sophia.

"And leave the board?"

They both looked at Michiko. She didn't know how to answer them. *Stay or go?* The spirit wasn't going anywhere, so they might as well look. But what if this was the wrong thing to do, and the spirit got angrier?

"Kokkuri-san, leave *now*," said Michiko. "We do not want you here." She hoped she was doing the right thing by being rude. She wished Hiro was by her side, guiding her—and then imagined he was. "You must leave!" she snapped.

A strong wind swirled through the room, swooping up loose bits of clothing and articles, and spinning them around. The three scattered. Right after, Michiko was flung backward so hard, she hit her head against the edge of the bed. Dazed, she sat there, knowing she'd made a horrible mistake. Kate and Sophia clung to each other. They didn't say a word but the stark horror on their faces was enough to make Michiko want to hurl.

This spirit was powerful. She seemed to have a presence that allowed her to manifest in her surroundings, away from the Ouija board. A potent stink of seaweed mixed with the smell of green tea hung in the room. The muttering grew louder, more distinct. Michiko could make out it was in Japanese, but, just like the last time, she didn't understand a single word. She stared helplessly at her friends, who both looked as white as the walls.

Now the coin came to life on the board, and all three started at the same time. It was moving fast—though none of them had a finger on it—spelling in a frenzy.

N-O-T-L-E-A-V-I- N-G

Kate jumped up and raced to the bathroom. The door slammed shut, and they heard her retching. Blind panic gnawed at Michiko as she sat frozen in place. The coin was now zipping across the board, spelling out another, familiar, word.

D-A-N-G-E-R

This spirit seems to be the only dangerous thing in the room! Michiko cried silently. *Is this the spirit's idea of a joke?* She touched the back of her sore head, staring at the board and praying for her cousin to call her back. The coin had stopped on the letter R, and the wind had died down just as abruptly as it had started.

"If the spirit can throw things around the room, she can, somehow, touch us—and much worse," hissed Sophia, glaring at Michiko. "*Someone* pushed me, and it's obvious it was the spirit." She looked close to tears. "But *why*? We didn't hurt or harm her in any way, so why is she punishing us? Has this ever happened before when you've played the Ouija board?"

Kate emerged from the bathroom, looking weak and pale. Michiko knew this was the time to tell the truth, no matter how painful, or at what cost. She forced herself to meet Sophia's and Kate's eyes and came out with it.

"I'm sorry. I don't have any answers to this. It's . . . it's the first time I've led a summoning."

Silence.

Sophia looked ready to explode. Kate turned even whiter than before. They looked angry and neither said a word to Michiko, who sat there feeling utterly miserable. She knew she deserved every bit of their anger. *What if she could never fix this?*

There was a knock on the door, making them jump. Michiko looked at her watch. It was almost 8 p.m. Where had the time gone? They should have been outside by now, to study the night sky.

"I'll go," said Michiko, wanting to get away from her friends' accusatory glares. She shoved the Ouija board under the bed, hurried to the door, and flung it open, trying to look calm despite her heart beating at triple speed.

Ms. Fraser stood outside, her lips a thin line and her eyes cold. "This is the *second* time today that you are all late to a group event. I thought I mentioned to everyone that we'll be studying the constellations because of the clear sky tonight and that we are all meeting at the entrance at 7:45 p.m. If you girls cannot keep an eye on the time, I will have to split you up and assign you to other rooms."

"I'm sorry, Ms. Fraser," said Michiko. "It won't happen again. We'll be right there."

"*So* humiliating," muttered Kate after the door was shut and Ms. Fraser had walked away. "It's as if we're kids, who need constant supervision."

"I know, right," said Sophia with a huff. "Everyone will wonder what we're up to. Let's just go."

They hurried out of the room without a glance at Michiko. She might have been invisible.

Michiko massaged her aching head. "Why, Kokkuri-san?" she whispered. "Why are you doing this? Why won't you leave us alone?"

Boo!

Michiko jumped at the whisper in her ear and whirled around. The smell of rotting seaweed was so strong, she almost gagged. K-san was close. *Very close.*

Wrenching open the door, she ran out. The sound of laughter followed her down the corridor and all the way to the cafeteria.

14

Most of the students were already outside, bundled up in their warm fleeces and hoodies, sipping hot chocolate. Michiko picked up a mug and walked out.

The night sky was truly spectacular. Not an inch of sky was devoid of shiny pinpricks of light. Michiko gazed up. She realized how small Earth was ... *she* was ... when compared to what was out there. The thought slowed down her racing heart.

"The best place to start is the Big Dipper," said Casey, pointing to the constellation with a laser. The beam cut through the night sky like a beacon. "It's not really a constellation, but part of one called the Ursa Major or the Great Bear, but because of its shape, you can find it easily."

"I can see the Ursa Minor!" said Karim.

Michiko wouldn't be surprised if he could point out all the constellations along with Casey. She looked to where Casey was now pointing out the stars beside the Dipper, which ended in the Polaris, or the North Star. Averting her eyes from the figures of Kate and Sophia at the far end of the line of students, she tried to follow along as Casey pointed out Orion the Hunter, Taurus, and the Gemini constellations. It was fascinating stuff, and some students were sketching in journals in the dark. Karim was one of them.

But all Michiko cared about was sending K-san back so that life could return to normal. If only she *could* turn back time.

"Why are you standing by yourself?" asked Sadia.

Michiko started, K-san's "prank" still fresh in her mind.

"Wow, you're jumpy," said Sadia with a quizzical look. "It's only me. Is everything all right?"

"I'm fine," lied Michiko. "We don't do everything in a group, you know." Even as she said it, her gut burned. Before this trip, she, Kate, and Sophia had *always* been together. *Had their friendship been so weak that one major problem had shown the cracks?*

"Right. Well, if you need any help or just to talk, I'm here," said Sadia.

Her voice was soft, even concerned, and it brought a lump to Michiko's throat. She'd judged Sadia without even knowing her that well, and how wrong she'd been! Yes, Sadia was overconfident, but she was also kind and perceptive. Michiko made a promise to herself: that she would never jump to conclusions about people without knowing the facts first.

"Thanks," said Michiko and moved to the back of the crowd, and far away from Ms. Fraser. She texted Mom to ask how she was doing. There was no reply, so she was probably asleep. She would call Dad tomorrow before they left for the morning excursion. By Friday noon, they would all be back on the bus, heading home. The only thing that brought her joy was that when she hugged Mom tomorrow, she wouldn't be worried that she would die. Mom was going to be okay. K-san had told her so, and she clung to that thought.

Suddenly, her phone pinged. It was Hiro, who was ready to chat.

Michiko slipped away to her room and shut the door. She would get into trouble if Ms. Fraser found out, but she was dealing with far scarier consequences right now.

The room was icy. The lamp flickered, and the air felt stagnant and heavy. K-san was still around. She would hear every word that Michiko said, and there was nothing she could do about it. Shuddering at the thought of K-san following them for the rest of their lives, she called Hiro using one of her free calling apps. He picked up immediately.

"How can I help, Cuz?" Hiro said.

The sound of his confident, unhurried voice calmed her. She told him everything. "I know I shouldn't have done it, but I had to know about Mom . . . and my friends wanted to know about Lucas," she added at the end.

Hiro let her finish without interrupting. "Don't beat yourself up too much, Miko. Spirits have been summoned for much less. Yes, it's a fun thing to do, but you also need a strong leader in the group. Spirits can sense weakness, you know that."

A bunch of screaming girls would appear weak, thought Michiko, but said nothing.

"You say the spirit keeps spelling the word 'danger' and refuses to leave?" said Hiro. "Hmmm, that's a new one for me."

"Sophia already tumbled down a sand dune. She swears someone pushed her. You think Kate is next? Or me?"

"I honestly don't know, Miko. Not unless I can see the board and ask a few questions of my own. The best advice I can give is to stay together and be alert. The spirit might get tired and leave. After all, there are so many people still using Ouija boards. If you're lucky, Kokkuri-san might answer someone else's call."

"Oh." Michiko's shoulders slumped. She had been so sure that Hiro would have a ready solution to get rid of the spirit. She was hoping for a chant or something that would force the spirit to go back. His advice didn't help at all, but she didn't say that out loud. She was already staying close to her friends, except that they wanted nothing to do with her.

"Will the coin go back to the torii gate once the spirit leaves?"

"It should," Hiro said. "But there will be other clues to let you know she has gone. For one, it won't be so cold in your room, nor will you keep sniffing out the distinctive rotten seaweed smell she comes with."

"Kate and Sophia are so mad at me," said Michiko glumly. "They barely talk to me anymore."

"That sucks," Hiro said. "Sorry to hear that, Miko, but you got this. Keep me posted about your mom. I want to know how she's doing and so does everyone here."

"Sure, thanks," said Michiko and hung up. She'd just had an idea, and she wanted to test it out.

Michiko peeked outside. The corridor was deserted. Everyone must still be watching the constellations. She closed the door and hurried to the Ouija board, which she had shoved under the bed when Ms. Fraser had knocked on the door. It wouldn't do for anyone else to find out about this, or they would all be in a lot of trouble.

Michiko sat cross-legged in front of the board and put both fingers on the coin. She knew that a minimum of two people were required, but maybe the spirit might let the rules go this time?

No maybes—she has to, she thought.

Her cousin had told her to take charge, and that's what Michiko would do.

15

"K-san, what do you want? Is there something I can help with? Tell me *why* you won't leave."

The coin stayed on R, reminding Michiko that the last word K-san had spelled out was danger.

So, that didn't work. "Okay, I need *your* help, Kokkuri-san."

The coin seemed to move the tiniest fraction.

She's listening!

Just then, the door to their room opened. Sophia and Kate came in, laughing. Their smiles faded as soon as they saw Michiko at the board. Kate slammed the door shut and turned around.

"You just can't leave it alone, can you?" said Kate. "You're so weird—I wish I'd never met you."

Her voice was so nasty, Michiko could only stare. The sweet, timid Kate was gone and whoever this was, she didn't like her at all. Sophia said nothing, barely glancing at Michiko. She was almost sure that their friendship was over. These two wouldn't forgive or forget.

"Our last night in this room," said Sophia. "Praise Santa Maria. I cannot wait to be in my room, alone."

"If only they had extra rooms at the lodge, we could have slept elsewhere," said Kate.

Neither of them made any attempt to keep their voices down. Michiko said nothing as they got into their beds. Folding the board and putting it back in the protective covering along with the coin, she reminded herself to focus on one thing only: sending the spirit back before they headed home tomorrow. A lump formed in her throat as she thought of the countless sleepovers they'd had. They'd be giggling and talking about everything under the sun until it actually came up, when sleep and exhaustion finally made them stop. That was all in the past now.

"Where's my toothbrush?" Sophia yelled from the bathroom.

Michiko and Kate both leaped off their beds and crowded into the bathroom. Only two brushes stood in the cup.

"Who took it?" Sophia questioned.

"Not me," said Kate,

"Me either," said Michiko.

They hunted high and low, before Michiko finally found it in the toilet bowl. It had sunk right to the bottom.

If Sophia were the Hindu god Shiva at that moment, Michiko would have turned into a pile of ash from the intensity of her gaze.

Without a word, Michiko left the room, found one of the staff members still cleaning the kitchen, and got a spare toothbrush for Sophia. Her friend snatched it from her hand without a word of thanks. K-san sure was relishing making her life miserable.

Finally, they all got into bed. Sophia read a book, while Kate was fast asleep in seconds. Michiko was dozing off too when they heard a soft knock on the door. Michiko jerked awake instantly, and her eyes met Sophia's. She looked petrified.

"Is that her?" whispered Sophia, her voice shaking. "Why won't she leave us alone?"

"She doesn't need to knock," said Michiko. "It's not her. I'll check. You stay."

Even though she was trembling on the inside, she forced herself to walk to the door. It was almost 11 p.m. *Who could it be at this hour?* Her first thought was about Mom. *Had there been an emergency and Dad had called Ms. Fraser instead of calling her?*

"Hey, you girls awake?" came a familiar voice. "I saw a light under the door and thought I'd check."

Lucas.

Michiko opened the door a crack, relief and anger flooding her. "What do you want?" she snapped. "You scared the crap out of us."

Lucas took a step back, running a hand through his hair and looking sheepish. "Sorry, Michiko. I couldn't sleep. What say we take a walk, get some night scenes of the desert, and sneak back? Sophia and Kate awake?"

Michiko stared at him. "Why don't you go with Sasha, like you did the other night?" Suddenly, she felt a burning sensation on her skin, almost like the time at the Kelso Dunes. As if the sun were scorching her. It was *so* odd to feel that at night, indoors.

"Dude's asleep already," said Lucas, his smile drooping. "Come on, it'll be fun. Or are you always a good little rule-follower?" His blue eyes looked like bottomless pools of black.

"I'll go," piped up Sophia behind her. Pulling on a

sweater over her PJs, she opened the door wide with a loud creak and smiled at Lucas. "I'm ready."

"Where are you guys going?" Kate called from her bed, sounding groggy.

"Lucas wants to go on a walk and take pictures," said Sophia. "It'll be cool. Coming, Kate?"

"We're not supposed to be outside," said Michiko in a quiet voice. "You know the rules. Snakes, scorpions, etc."

"Thanks, *Mom*," said Sophia with a sneer. "But I think you've looked after us quite enough."

Michiko felt her face grow warm and her insides twist. Lucas was watching them all intently, but he still stood there. If only he'd leave, she wouldn't have to do what she was about to.

Kate, wearing a hoodie, had joined them at the door. "Hey, Lucas."

"Hi, Kate, you coming? She's out." His chin jerked toward Michiko.

"Lead on," said Kate.

"Right behind you," said Sophia.

Michiko took a deep breath and steeled herself. "If any of you step out the front door, I'm waking Ms. Fraser and Casey, right now," she said. "It's not safe and I won't let you do it." She had to keep her friends safe until she figured out what other dangers were in store for them.

Sophia and Kate scoffed and shook their heads at her. Lucas gave a low, mean laugh. "Who would have thought you'd turn out to be a boring sneak?" The two girls broke out into laughter.

Michiko held her ground, arms crossed, glaring at them. Inside she was cringing. Dying.

"You won't really snitch on us, will you?" asked Sophia, taking a step closer to Lucas.

"Try me," said Michiko, her voice cold. She had to make them see sense and if it meant being rude, so be it.

"She's serious," hissed Kate, throwing her a disgusted look.

"Maybe we can get together when we're back home, Lucas. Right, Kate?" Sophia smiled at Kate, who nodded vigorously.

"You got it." Lucas winked at Sophia and Kate. It was as if all three were in a bubble and Michiko was outside it. Or just invisible. "'Nite, ladies," he said and walked away.

With the lights finally out and the sound of Kate's and Sophia's deep breathing filling the still air, Michiko cried silently into her pillow. In her heart, she knew she'd done the right thing. Even if it meant she no longer had the best friends she was trying so hard to protect.

16

Michiko switched off the blaring alarm she'd set the night before so they would not be late for breakfast again. Her bed was closest to the window, and she lay still for a minute, taking in the wispy clouds—the streaks of orange. A flock of birds, silhouetted against the lightening sky, flew by in a V formation. As the events of the last two days gradually flooded her head, a weight settled on her chest.

She sat up, her eyes roving the dark room. The pockets of shadow seemed ominous. What did K-san have in store for them today? As she dressed, she chanted to herself, over and over, *stay strong.* The room still felt cold, but it could just as easily be the chilly desert morning rather than a lingering spirit from the world of the dead. Michiko hoped that was all it was.

Kate and Sophia hadn't stirred despite the alarm and the lights. Michiko shook them awake.

"Cafeteria in thirty minutes," she said. "Hurry if you don't want Ms. Fraser calling us out again."

Neither said a word as they stirred awake. Sophia was the first one into the bathroom. Kate lay under the covers, her back to Michiko. She'd always been the kinder one, so it stung even more to see her so aloof.

"I will make this right," said Michiko. "You can count on it. Just be vigilant today, Kate. Please?"

No response.

Michiko picked up her hoodie and walked out. She'd be alert for all three of them.

The cafeteria staff had almost finished setting up by the time she walked in. The fragrance of bacon, hash browns, and eggs filled the air. Casey was at a table eating breakfast as she scrolled through her phone.

"Morning!" she called out cheerily when she saw Michiko.

"Hey!" Michiko replied.

"Get some breakfast and join me," Casey said.

Michiko helped herself to some eggs, hash browns and hot chocolate, and joined Casey at her table.

"Where are your roommates?" Casey asked.

"Getting ready," said Michiko. Every time someone mentioned her friends, it felt like two hard jabs to the chest.

"You look down," said Casey. "Everything all right?"

"Sure," replied Michiko, taking a large bite of hash browns and egg. She chewed slowly so she wouldn't have to answer with her mouth full. She hoped Casey would take the hint and not grill her about anything.

"How is Sophia feeling now?" Casey asked. "That was quite a tumble. Good thing we were just on the dunes. Odd, though, that she would trip over her laces. As far as I recall, her shoes didn't have any. I didn't want to point it out in front of everyone, especially since she was terrified."

Casey was smart and observant. Nothing seemed to get past her.

"What *really* happened?" Casey eyed her shrewdly. "Did

someone push her, or did she stumble and was too embarrassed to admit it?"

Michiko took a sip of hot chocolate wondering how to answer Casey and also put a stop to more questions. "She's fine now, really. Er . . . what are we doing today?"

Casey looked at Michiko for a long moment, as if she knew Michiko was keen to change the subject, but, thankfully, she asked no more questions about Sophia.

"We'll explore the Lava Tube," said Casey. "It's short and manageable. You'll see a shaft of light once you reach the interior of the cave. Great photo op."

"Sounds good," said Michiko. Her heart thudded as she thought about being in a dark, underground cave with the unspoken dangers promised by K-san.

Most of the students had trickled into the cafeteria, but Kate and Sophia still hadn't made an appearance. Michiko glanced at her watch.

"Your friends will be here," said Casey. "We still have plenty of time."

Michiko looked surprised. *Did she miss anything?*

Casey laughed. "Yes, I'm very observant, but it's second nature to me. This place teaches you to respect the outdoors. Every movement could be a potential disaster waiting to happen. I also spent time in Australia. It has some of the deadliest insects and animals on the planet. If you're not vigilant, it could be fatal."

"Thanks, we'll all be super careful," Michiko replied. "So, just the Lava Tube before we head home?"

"We'll also hike the Rings Loop Trail," said Casey, finishing the last of her coffee and wiping her mouth with a napkin. "It's fun, and you'll see some amazing rock formations before you head back home. See you later."

Michiko smiled as Casey touched her lightly on the

shoulder and walked away with her empty plate and coffee mug.

As she left the cafeteria, Sophia and Kate walked in. Michiko, out of habit, raised her arm and waved them over to her empty table. They saw her and Kate stopped, moving to take a step toward the waiting Michiko. Before she could even lower her arm, Sophia steered Kate away to another table.

Michiko's hurt turned to anger. *So be it.*

17

By 9 o'clock, everyone was outside the lodge, ready to explore the Lava Tube and tackle the hike. A shuttle would take them to the trailhead for the tube. Casey had explained that there was a short walk to the steps leading down to the tube.

"Once you get to the end of the cave, there's a perfect spot for pictures where a shaft of sunlight comes in," said Casey. "The cave itself isn't too deep, so feel free to explore. Then we head to the Rings Loop Trail, also called the Hole-in-the Wall Trail. It's 1.3 miles and not too difficult, but you'll see some spectacular rock formations.

"What's the trail rating?" Sadia asked.

"You must be a hiker," said Casey with a smile. "It's rated as moderate and starts out very flat. Some of the steeper sections have rings attached to help you pull yourselves up. And I'll be there to help. Now ..."

As Casey went on, Michiko stood listening by herself. Kate and Sophia were still a threesome but now it was Lucas who tagged along wherever they went, sticking to them like superglue. *He'd never been this interested in them before, so why was he swooping in to steal her friends now?* Michiko turned her face away from the chattering trio. She tried to squash her feelings of jealousy, admitting to herself that with Lucas close by, at least he might be able to help if either of them was in trouble. She decided to keep an eye on them, but from a distance.

"He's giving me the cold shoulder too," someone whispered.

Sadia stood beside her, looking bummed. "I thought Lucas was a good friend. Suddenly, we're not, and his besties are now *your* ex-best friends. Weird trip, huh? What say we don't give a hoot and hang out?"

Michiko couldn't agree more. "Sure has been. Let's do it. I'm looking forward to the hike."

She used to go hiking with Hiro back in Japan. Her favorite had been the hike up Mt. Fuji, Japan's tallest mountain, only to be attempted during the hiking season of July and August. It had been a tough and grueling hike but totally worth the effort once they got to the top. As was customary, she'd stamped her hiking stick at one of the stations and sent a postcard to herself back in the States. It had been waiting for her when she returned. Kate and Sophia preferred malls to mountains. *Quit it*, she interrupted her thoughts. Sadia was right—she had to stop thinking about her ex-best friends.

"Me too!" said Sadia, her eyes sparkling. "The Rings Loop is supposed to be super fun! I saw a short documentary about it, and I can't wait to try it!"

At this Michiko beamed. "I saw it too—on YouTube, right?"

Sadia nodded. "Finally, we get a real workout."

How had she ever thought Sadia was horrible without getting to know her? She was pretty cool and liked at least one thing that she did. Maybe she could make a new friend and salvage this cursed trip, after all.

They sat beside each other on the bus, watching the desert scenery go by. The squat and spiky Joshua trees seemed to wave out to them as they sped toward the Lava Tube. The scrub and bushes looked gray and colorless, but Michiko hadn't forgotten that there were hundreds of small but deadly creatures hiding under them during the day, only to emerge when it got cooler.

"Oh, did you see that jackrabbit?" said Michiko, pointing to a clump of bushes.

"Yup!" said Sadia, leaning across Michiko for a better look. "I'd like to smuggle one home with me. Do you think Ms. Fraser would mind?"

Michiko nodded, smirking. "It's *Casey* you need to watch out for. She loves this place and every single thing in it."

Sadia smiled. "In that case, I better drop the idea."

A loud laugh from the back of the bus caught their attention. Michiko turned around to see Sophia grinning while Lucas guffawed at some private joke.

"Just ignore them," said Sadia. "Lucas likes to laugh extra loud even when something's not too funny. It's just his way of drawing attention to himself. At first, I thought it was cute. Now it only irritates me."

The shuttle stopped at the trailhead. Ms. Fraser stood up at the front of the bus with Casey beside her.

"We're here," said Casey cheerfully. "It's a half-mile walk to the ladder before we descend into the Lava Tube. Please bring your caps and water bottles. Make sure you've put on sunscreen and if you haven't, I have a couple of extra bottles with me. The sun is harsh, so make sure you protect your skin."

"Watch out for snakes and scorpions," added Ms. Fraser anxiously. "No wandering off the path, you lot!"

"Yes, Ms. Fraser!" they said in unison.

Gravel crunched beneath Michiko's feet, and the warm air smelled of wet earth and dry rock. After the chill in her room, the heat felt good on her skin. Sadia fell into step beside her as they walked. Lucas was at the back with Kate and Sophia. Sasha was with some other classmates. It looked as if they'd both had a change of friends. Michiko tried hard to tune out their voices as she took pictures of the stark landscape around her. Everyone was clicking away. The sun rose higher in the sky, which had turned a brilliant blue with faint brushstrokes of wispy clouds.

It was so beautiful that Michiko stopped to take a selfie. She'd text it to Mom and Dad and ask how they were doing. Just as she tapped the screen, Sophia, Kate, and Lucas photobombed her. She whirled around and they hurried away, laughing.

Seriously? Michiko tried not to let their childish behavior get her down as she hurried to catch up to Sadia. They had reached the mouth of the Lava Tube and were about to go down the ladder.

"Careful," said Casey. "This ground does not make for a soft landing. You fall and you'll be badly hurt." Her eyes swept the group and seemed to linger on Sophia for a few seconds before moving on.

"Let's go," said Ms. Fraser. "We want to finish this and Rings Loop Trail by noon. Then we hit the road, so we're back home by late afternoon."

As Michiko climbed down the ladder, the temperature dropped. Within minutes, they were all on the ground and looking toward the narrow mouth of the tube, formed by molten lava years ago. Michiko felt a moment of panic when she saw how small the entrance was, barely three feet high.

"Do we have to crawl through that all the way?" she asked. "I'm ... claustrophobic."

Casey shook her head. "It gets a lot bigger once you're past that section. You'll be able to stand for most of the way. We'll go to the very end, where the shaft of sunlight falls into the cave and then back again."

Casey went first to show how it was done. One by one, they all followed. Michiko hesitated, but Sadia reached out a hand and helped her through.

Bent over, they crawled a few feet into the cave. It got darker, and the air felt thicker. Michiko forced herself to take deep breaths, putting one foot in front of the other. The air had a damp but clean smell to it, and yet Michiko felt trapped as her fingertips brushed the jagged rocks on either side of her. Finally, the ceiling got higher, and they were all able to stand upright. Michiko breathed a sigh of relief and swiped her sleeve across her forehead.

Flashes from phone cameras went off intermittently as Casey pointed out interesting features. Sadia and Michiko took a selfie in the warm buttery sunlight pouring in from the hole in the roof, or natural skylight, as it was also called. Kate, Sophia, and Lucas waited their turn. There was one spot at the end of the tube that was just right for a photo op, and everyone wanted a picture right there.

"Hey, Michiko!"

It was Sophia. Michiko's heart leaped into her mouth. *Had they finally forgiven her?* She whirled back with an expectant look while Sadia wandered away.

But her face fell when she saw Sophia holding out her

phone with the purple case. The case had a heart on it, in which were her and Kate's initials.

"Please take a picture of the three of us?" she said, smiling sweetly.

"*Two* of us," said Lucas, and stepped aside. "You don't want me ruining it."

"We do!" Kate and Sophia piped in.

Lucas ignored them and moved into the shadows. As Michiko took the phone from Sophia, she saw his eyes flash red in the darkness. She blinked, and they looked normal again. It must have been a trick of the light. Blue eyes turning blood red? She had to admit she was fixating on Lucas. Was it jealousy because he'd stolen her friends, or that he was an odd duck and she'd only noticed it now?

"Hurry!" said Sophia.

Michiko turned back to her friends. They were smiling, but not at her. She swallowed the lump in her throat and wordlessly clicked a couple of pictures.

"Want me to take one of the three of you?" Casey asked, coming up behind Michiko.

"We're good, thanks," said Sophia, plucking the phone from Michiko's hand and tucking it into her pocket.

Kate gave a tentative smile, and they walked away. Casey looked at Michiko. "Looks like you guys have had a falling out. Anything I can do to help?"

Yes, send back a spirit we called using the Ouija board, so she stops scaring us. "Thanks, but they're just being weird. They'll snap out of it when we get home."

A student called out for Casey. She patted Michiko on the back and hurried away.

Michiko's throat was tight as she walked unaccompanied along the Lava Tube toward the ladder. She was close to bawling. How easy it had been for Kate and Sophia to bury their friendship, she thought. She kept to the shadows, peering at the red stone streaked with brown and black.

As Michiko passed by an alcove, a single whispered word made the hair on her neck stand up.

Danger!

18

K-san was right here.

Michiko suppressed a scream as she peered into the shadows, looking for the spirit she couldn't shake off. "Go back and leave us alone!" she whispered, hoping none of the students or the teacher could hear her. They would think she had gone mad.

There was no reply. Her breath fogged in front of her face, and she could feel something poking at her subconscious. As if K-san was trying to tell her something.

"Just tell me what you want and I'll do it," Michiko said. "Because of you, my friends won't talk to me anymore."

Not good friends, came a hoarse, raspy voice that sounded a million years old.

The spirit had a point, but Michiko wasn't about to have a discussion with a spirit who could push someone down a dune and continue to scare them.

"Will you please leave us alone?" Michiko asked wearily.

Her own breath, exhaled into the dark alcove, formed two letters: N-O.

Michiko backed out of the alcove just as Sadia came up

to her. "Where have you been? We're leaving. You don't want to be left behind, and I know you need help to get out of that narrow section. Hurry!"

Michiko hugged herself tightly. Being left behind in a dark cave with K-san would be a nightmare.

"Thanks for coming back for me, Sadia!" she said and smiled with gratitude. "You're awesome."

"Don't go all emo on me!" Sadia linked arms with her, and they raced to catch up with the other students, who'd started to climb the ladder to the top. Just before she squeezed through the narrow section of the cave, Michiko looked back.

In the darkness hovered the same old lady in the kimono she'd seen before. The old woman was grinning maniacally, her mouth a bloody slash. To think *this* was in their room every night, watching while they slept, made her want to barf. The possibility of bringing her back home and never being rid of her sent a jolt through Michiko.

She whimpered and almost jumped through the gap. "Ow!" she yelped as a sharp pain ripped through her forearm, which had caught on a jagged piece of rock. But she scrambled on. Then she was through and hurrying toward the ladder.

"You've cut yourself," said Sadia, and called out, "does anyone have a Band-Aid?"

"Later," said Michiko. "Let's get to the bus. Hurry!"

"Hold up, are you okay? You look like someone's chasing you," said Sadia, glancing back into the tube. "There's no one there. Do you think someone's playing tricks? Is it Lucas?"

Someone is playing with me, but not Lucas, thought Michiko. "It's nothing," she said out loud. "I think I might have heard the rattle of a Mojave green."

Sadia said nothing. Once they climbed onto the bus, she asked Casey, "Do we have a first-aid kit? Michiko has cut herself."

"Yes, we do," said Casey. "Sit down and I'll clean it up while we head to the hike."

Kate and Sophia had seen the gash on Michiko's arm, but neither said a word as Casey cleaned the cut and put a Band-Aid on it. Lucas came over to watch.

"Bumped yourself in the dark there, Michiko?" said Lucas, sniffling.

"If you've got a cold coming on, you'd better keep your distance," said Casey, not looking up from what she was doing. "We don't want to catch what you have."

Lucas blushed and backed away. "I just wanted to help."

After Casey returned to the front of the bus, he circled back and sat beside Michiko. "Are you okay? I am so sorry you're hurt. Is it a deep cut? May I see it?" He almost sounded excited.

"Calm down, dude," said Sadia. "It's only a cut, not a hemorrhage."

"It's covered up," said Michiko. "And no, it isn't too deep."

"Well, I hope you feel better soon," he said with a sniff. Lucas's eyes—now blue—gazed into hers, and he seemed genuinely concerned. It helped a little to know that even though her best friends were deliberately ignoring her, Lucas still looked like he cared.

"Weirdo," said Sadia once Lucas had rejoined Sophia and Kate at the back of the bus. "Excited about a minor cut. Boys, am I right?" She rolled her eyes, making Michiko laugh.

"I could do without some of them," Michiko added, and Sadia smiled knowingly.

The bus stopped in the parking lot ringed by cliffs of rock. Casey stood up and explained what they were about to see and the safety rules.

"This one's totally doable by you guys," Casey said with a smile, her gaze sweeping them all. "Remember to use the metal rings attached to the rock when you're climbing through the crevasses. Some sections are steep, and you do *not* want to twist an ankle here."

Someone broke the silence. "Um . . . may I stay back?" asked Kate. "I'm not a good hiker and heights scare me."

"Nonsense," Ms. Fraser replied. "If *I* can do it, you can all manage it. As Casey said, just be careful. And look where you step. That goes without saying. We'll help each other if anyone gets stuck. Right?"

There was a chorus of yeses.

Casey took the lead and Ms. Fraser brought up the rear. They all trooped out of the bus, which seemed tiny when surrounded by the massive boulders around them. They were full of holes—some the size of a car, as if a giant had punched them in a fit of anger, and some small enough for a child to curl up in. The sun had climbed to its zenith, and the air smelled dusty. There was another underlying smell that Michiko couldn't identify. Gasps filled the air as everyone gazed around in awe.

"Everyone got their water bottles?" Casey asked. "If anyone needs a refill, do it now. We have a large container on the bus, so help yourselves. You must stay hydrated even though it's a short hike. Especially since it's warm."

"I'm really not comfortable with this," said Kate, pinching her lower lip nervously. "May I stay on the bus and read?" The bright sunshine shone off her pale face.

Michiko felt sorry for her. Neither she nor Sophia was outdoorsy, but Kate had known what she was signing up for;

all the trip's activities had been listed on the notice sent home. Was she nervous about the hike . . . or K-san and what she might do to her? Kate's eyes met hers momentarily and slid away, but it was enough for Michiko to see the fear in them.

"Don't be silly, Kate," said Ms. Fraser. "This is an opportunity of a lifetime. You'll be a better hiker only if you try. We're all here to help you."

"I'll help you," Lucas said. "Trust me, I won't be far off."

Sadia elbowed Michiko at that with a smirk, which she ignored. Her ears had perked up at what Sophia had just chimed in.

"You know I got your back, girl."

Sophia would use that line often, for them both. Now Michiko was out, and Lucas was in.

At least some good had come to her ex-best friends from playing the Ouija board. They'd wanted to know whom Lucas liked best, and now they had their answer.

19

"Stay on the path and keep an eye out for snakes," said Casey as they started down the flat trail toward the cliffs. "It's too hot for them to be out at this time of day, but there are pockets of shade along the way. They might be resting there. Be vigilant." She walked through a gap in the barbed wire fence and toward the trailhead.

Chattering excitedly, the group followed Casey in a line as she pointed out interesting cacti, desert flowers, and the tracks of scorpions, spiders, and snakes on the sandy patches. It was fascinating how much Casey could see and hear in their surroundings. Now her attention to detail made sense. Even from the middle of the line, Michiko saw Casey sweeping the landscape ahead of her as they made their way over to geological formations in the desert.

Only a few students separated Kate, Sophia, and Lucas from her and Sadia. Michiko made sure to stay close behind so she could keep an eye on the trio, all the while wishing K-san had been more precise with her predictions.

After walking over some large boulders that needed your full attention, they came to the first crevasse. It was narrow and steep, but there were rings along the path so climbers could pull themselves up. One by one, they made their way to the top. An overenthusiastic Karim almost got stuck, and Casey had to come down and help him climb up the narrow path. Red-faced and sweaty, he finally made it to the top and gave a whoop of joy.

"This is so cool!" he said, throwing his arms out as if trying to hug the world.

Some students laughed. Lucas called out to him, "You're pretty cool yourself."

Despite her fear, Kate also managed the climb to the top of the first boulder with lots of encouragement from Sophia. In front of her, Lucas reached out a hand to help her now and then. The three were having so much fun, it seemed like that they'd forgotten she'd ever been part of their group.

"Don't pay any attention to them," Sadia said to Michiko once they'd made it. "They'll come around when Lucas tires of them and moves on to the next group of friends. He likes variety. He's hardly spending time with Sasha, who used to be his shadow. Didn't you notice?"

Now that she mentioned it, Michiko realized she was spot on. She looked around for Sasha and found him chatting with Karim. *Odd.* Only two nights ago, he and Lucas had been goofing around together. "You're right, who cares about them? This view, though, is to die for!"

From their vantage point, they had a clear view of the Mojave Desert and the Banshee Canyon. It was beautiful, even in its starkness. Joshua trees dotted the landscape of shrub and cacti. Now and then some small animal scurried along the ground, but otherwise, the landscape seemed devoid of life.

"The desert is deserted," said Sadia with a grin.

"Don't be fooled," said Casey, taking a swig of water.

"The desert is *teeming* with life just under the surface. Insects and small animals are hiding in caves, under rocks, anywhere the sun cannot reach. Once the sun sets, they'll be out hunting for food. Never wander out at night in this or any desert unless you have the right gear, plenty of light, and a knowledgeable guide."

Michiko's eyes darted to Lucas, the serial rulebreaker. He'd gone out with Sasha the first night, but, luckily, nothing bad had happened. Last night, he'd invited Kate and Sophia. The only reason they hadn't been out was because she'd put her foot down. Listening to Casey's repeated warning, she was glad she'd been firm. If she hadn't, who knows what desert creatures might have attacked them?

The desert! Suddenly she made the connection. *This* was the danger K-san was talking about—the desert. It made perfect sense. How had it taken her so long to connect the dots? That Casey and K-san had been warning them about the same dangers this whole time! Michiko almost laughed out loud as instant relief flooded her. She only had to be vigilant and stay safe until they reached home. Finally, she'd figured out why the spirit had been lingering, and when she would leave them alone.

"Wait for me!" she called to Sadia and hurried over.

With a spring in her step now, Michiko kept pace with Sadia as the group kept going.

"The first time I hiked with my cousin, I was so ill-equipped," said Michiko, feeling chatty. "I wore the wrong shoes, didn't eat a good breakfast, and wasn't carrying enough water."

"Mistakes are the best teachers, am I right?" said Sadia. "I got severe cramps on one hike due to dehydration. I was hiking the Black Mountain Trail via Rhus Ridge. I always carry a couple of bottles of water before I set out now. And drink at least a gallon before starting off."

"I'd love to do that one with you when we get back home," said Michiko.

"You bet!" said Sadia.

They carefully wound their way down a narrow path strewn with loose gravel and stones, trying to keep their balance. It was hot work. Michiko wiped her forehead with her wristband and took a large gulp of water. The sun was directly overhead and beat down on their heads with ferocity. A scorching wind blew across the desert and tumbleweed rolled across the sandy floor. Michiko's eyes watered from the grit, and she was so sweaty, she wanted to jump in a cold shower.

"How much longer?" Karim asked. Red-faced, with large sweat stains around his armpits, he seemed to be suffering the most.

"We're at the halfway mark," said Casey. "A little farther up there's a shady spot where we can take a break, recharge, and eat an energy bar. It'll give you a boost. Once we finish the loop, you'll be on your way home in an air-conditioned bus and you're going to miss this gorgeous heat. Trust me!"

Karim huffed noisily. "I don't think so," he said, while his friends laughed.

Michiko's heart went out to him. She slipped up beside Karim and handed him her energy bar. "It's not much, but the sugar will help until we make the next stop."

"You sure?" Karim asked, eyeing the bar.

Michiko nodded, and Karim downed the bar in two bites. "Thanks," he said. "This is so hard."

Ten minutes later, they came up to another crevasse. This one was steeper than the previous one, and just as narrow. The only good thing was that it was short. The eight metal rings hammered into the side of the boulder would be useful to pull themselves up.

"Okay, people," said Casey, stopping at the foot of the crevasse. "We're doing this one at a time. I do not want the next person to follow unless the person in front of you has reached the top. We do not want a traffic jam or anyone panicking. We take it slow. Clear?"

Everyone agreed.

"Ms. Fraser, please send one student up at a time. Lucas can climb up with me and help as needed. I'll talk them through it in case anyone gets stuck."

"Sounds like a plan," their teacher said, though, when she thought no one was looking, she made a sign of the cross, staring worriedly at the crevasse. Michiko could understand her nervousness. She had twenty students to look after, and not all were in good physical shape. For those who hadn't hiked or scrambled before, this must have looked daunting, even though it was rated as moderate. Not only did you need strength in your legs, but you needed upper body strength too. Luckily, Michiko had done so many hikes with her cousins, especially Hiro, that this was a piece of cake.

"Don't worry," said Michiko to Karim when she noticed how worried he looked. "It's easy once you begin. Look before you step, test your foothold, and pull yourself up using the metal rings."

Karim nodded as Kate started the climb before them, babbling uncontrollably. Michiko knew it was nervousness.

As she looked up toward Kate, her skin started to burn, the same way it had on the dunes. Again, the sky seemed to darken. She couldn't take her eyes off her friend as she climbed gingerly, K-san's warnings pulsing in Michiko's head like a lighthouse beacon.

20

Kate's scream the next minute pierced Michiko's heart and cut through the chatter of students awaiting their turn. Then it stopped abruptly, which was even more worrying.

Everyone crowded the base of the crevasse, craning their heads. Kate was at the halfway point, immobile.

"What's the matter, Kate?" Ms. Fraser called up to her. "Don't be scared if you're stuck. Take a deep breath—"

"S-snake," Kate blurted out.

"Kate, FREEZE!" said Casey from the top of the crevasse. Her voice sounded calm despite the next words. "It's a Mojave green."

Muffled gasps of horror and confusion went around the gathered students. Ms. Fraser looked ready to pass out. Michiko watched helplessly, fighting every instinct to race up the crevasse right after her terrified friend, who was face to face with a poisonous rattlesnake.

"Do you want me to chase it away, or what?" Lucas said.

Michiko stared at him. He didn't sound concerned at all. *Did he even understand the gravity of the situation?*

"Why didn't I see it when I came up?" said Casey, more

to herself than anyone else. "The rock is too hot for it to be out. Something seems to have disturbed it—"

"Casey, this is no time for a biology lesson," said Ms. Fraser, her voice trembling. "What do we do? I don't want any of my students bitten!"

"Wait it out," said Casey. "The best thing is to let the snake have some space. It will probably crawl away on its own when it sees no threat. So, everyone, stay *very* still." After a pause, she added to Ms. Fraser, "And I have the antidote, should she get bitten."

The silence was deafening, except for a tiny whimper that Michiko was sure came from Kate. Two minutes crawled by, then five. The students murmured among themselves, but Michiko couldn't take her eyes off her friend who seemed to be trembling but trying very hard to stay still. K-san had warned them of danger and now here it was, staring at Kate and shaking its rattle at her. *But how could they have prevented it?* They had all followed Casey's instructions, so how could anyone have predicted *this*?

It grew hotter. Sweat pooled in Michiko's armpits. It felt like entire hours had gone by in a span of minutes. She glanced at Sophia, who stood beside Ms. Fraser, white-faced and livid. Their eyes met and Michiko walked over to her, pulling her aside so they wouldn't be overheard.

"She'll be okay—" Michiko whispered.

"Shut up," Sophia cut her off in a low but gruff voice. She dragged Michiko farther away from the students. Not that it mattered, because all eyes and ears were riveted to Kate, who seemed to be frozen in that crevasse, her right hand still clutching the metal ring beside her.

"This is *your* fault," Sophia said through gritted teeth. "That spirit warned us of danger because she was planning to hurt us, one by one. How could you even suggest something so dangerous? I thought we were best friends?" Sophia's voice shook as she glanced at Kate and back again. "How could you do this to us?"

"Please believe me," said Michiko, glad that Sophia was talking to her, even if it was only angry words. "This was not supposed to happen. I've been part of many Ouija summonings and all of them were fun. The spirit answered a few questions and went away."

"But this was your first time alone, which you kept from us," said Sophia. "You could easily have called the wrong spirit. Or forgotten a step—"

Suddenly, something clattered behind them and landed on the ground with a thump. They both whirled around. It was only a stone that had landed nearby. They both looked at each other and ran back toward their classmates.

"Oops!" said Lucas as an ominous rattling filled the silence. "My foot hit a loose stone."

Kate screamed and the rattling sound became louder, still louder.

Suddenly, the snake leaped into the air and flew backwards. It was silhouetted against the clear blue sky for a second before it dropped out of sight among the boulders. The rattling stopped abruptly. Kate crumpled on the spot.

"KATE!" yelled Casey, scrambling down to help her.

Michiko charged ahead, pushing Ms. Fraser aside. She was up the crevasse, climbing as fast as she could. She reached her friend at the same time as Casey, just as an unconscious Kate let go of the metal ring. Her face was so pale, it was almost translucent.

Michiko pulled out the water bottle from her backpack and pressed it to Kate's colorless lips. "You're safe, Kate. Please wake up. Here, take a sip."

Ms. Fraser had clambered up too, grunting with the

exertion, and peered over Michiko's shoulder. "Is she okay? Oh my God, my heart. If she'd been bitten, what would I have told her parents?" She looked pale too and Casey thrust her own water bottle at her.

"Everyone, calm down," said Casey. She must have realized that if Ms. Fraser panicked or broke down, so would the students. "We're all okay," she called out to the group waiting at the bottom. "Let's cut this short and head back to the bus. Stay where you are, and we'll all be right down."

Not long after, Kate opened her eyes and took a sip of the water, then a gulp. Color flooded her cheeks. "I'm okay," she said softly. "Can we please go home?"

"That's the plan," said Casey. She turned around and called to Lucas, who was still crouched on the rock above, looking down at them. "You can follow once we're all down. Be careful and keep an eye out. There could be a snake nest here, which explains why we saw one in the afternoon." She paused, her mouth tightening grimly. "And don't be careless again. Dislodging that stone could have had serious consequences."

Michiko looked up at Lucas. He didn't seem in the least bit upset or shaken that, because of his carelessness, he'd almost got a student bitten by a venomous snake.

It was hard to see with the sun in her eyes, but she was almost certain he was smiling.

21

The bus ride back home was subdued compared to when they'd set out for this field trip. Students still sat in their groups, but they talked in low voices or whispers as they ate the packed lunches provided by Casey and the staff at the preserve. Ms. Fraser had insisted that Kate lie down on the back seat.

"I need a full account of this," Ms. Fraser said, looking grim, "so I can report this to the principal and then to your parents."

"No!" Kate wailed. "They'll never let me go on another trip again. I'm fine now, so can we please forget about it? Please?"

Ms. Fraser shook her head. "I'm afraid not, Kate. It is the school's policy to report all incidents concerning students to their parents. We cannot just forget about it. This is so we can keep you safe on the next school trip. Let's get started."

Finally, Kate gave her all the details. Sophia sat beside her, clutching her hand. Michiko sat a seat away, listening carefully. She needed to know exactly what had happened.

"How did the snake leap backward?" Ms. Fraser asked,

looking perplexed. "I've never seen a snake do that before. In fact, it might have defied the laws of physics and nature!"

Kate shrugged. "I don't know."

"Lucky for us," said Ms. Fraser with a shudder.

Once she had recorded all the facts on her phone, she went to the front of the bus. Michiko was alone with Sophia and Kate at the back, with the closest students a few seats away. With the sound of the bus's engine, she was sure no one would overhear them. She had to tell them her theory about the desert being the harbinger of danger, if only they'd listen.

"I'm so sorry about what happened, Kate," Michiko began.

Kate looked away. Michiko felt her confidence draining like water from a sieve. But she had to get through to her friends. She took a deep breath and continued.

"I have a theory."

"No, thanks," said Kate, her green eyes locking with Michiko's. They were full of bitter anger. "Your friendship will be the death of us."

There was a lump of hurt in Michiko's throat. *How could they blame her for a snake appearing in the wilderness, which was its natural habitat?* It could have happened to any of them. Michiko opened her mouth, but no words came out. She had to admit that it *hadn't* happened to anyone else. It had happened to *Kate*. And the first accident had happened to Sophia.

Before she could say anything else, Lucas joined them at the back of the bus, looking slightly less cheerful than he seemed atop the crevasse.

"You okay, Kate?" he asked. "You were awesome! I could *never* have stood so still faced with a venomous snake! How did you do it?"

Kate shrugged, blushing. Sophia put an arm around her friend's shoulders, immediately perking up. "We do what we have to do to survive, right? When the going gets tough, the tough get going."

Michiko almost rolled her eyes at the cliché. But she had a question for Lucas.

"How could you have been so careless as to dislodge that stone, Lucas?" Michiko asked, watching his face carefully. In all the anxiety over Kate, everyone had overlooked his role in the incident. "You startled the snake. It could easily have bitten Kate if not for the fact that it flew in the opposite direction, which is another mystery."

Lucas hung his head. "I'm so sorry. I was so worried about Kate that I wasn't paying attention to my surroundings and didn't notice that stone under my foot. Before I could stop it, the stone fell." His eyes were moist, and he looked like he was going to cry as he held Kate's gaze. "You believe me, right? You know I would never harm you deliberately."

Michiko was horrified. His explanation seemed to make perfect sense.

Sophia awkwardly patted Lucas on the shoulder. "Of course, we believe you. We know what might have caused this, and it wasn't *you*."

"Really?" said Lucas. He glanced at all of them, his eyes coming to rest on Sophia. "Tell me what's going on and I can help."

"None of your business, Lucas," Michiko piped in. "Can you give us some privacy, please?"

Lucas gave her an odd look, almost angry. In the depths of his blue eyes was a glimmer of that old red flash, but it was gone in a second. He stood up and walked away without a word, just as a brief searing pain prickled her skin, like a sunburn. Kate and Sophia shifted in the next seat, awkwardly complaining about the desert heat they'd already left behind.

Michiko's brain felt like a blender. So many questions and theories whirled inside, to which she had no answers.

22

"You're pathetic!" Sophia said after Lucas was out of earshot. "You caused this mess, and now you're jealous because Lucas is friends with us. Who are you, and what have you done with *our* Michiko?"

"Hear me out!" said Michiko. "Please."

"Scared that it's *your* turn soon?" said Kate, all timidness and hesitation from her voice gone. "You started this and now you have to face the consequences. You *deserve* whatever happens to you."

"Leave us alone, or we're leaving," Sophia said. Her face looked like it was made of granite. "We don't want to be friends with you anymore, if it wasn't clear already. Don't talk to us."

"Ever again," Kate added. They sat as one, glaring at her.

Michiko stood up and walked to an empty seat midway down the bus. A beautiful landscape rushed past, but Michiko barely noticed. There was no doubt in her mind now that she'd lost both her best friends at the same time. There was no chance either of them would forgive her after the accident with Kate. Not after all the awful words they'd

POSSESSED

uttered with conviction to Michiko recently. She'd never even thought the two of them were capable of being so mean.

Just before the school bus pulled into the parking lot, she sent off a text to Hiro.

Gotta talk to you. On my way home from the field trip.

As the bus rolled to a stop, Michiko saw her dad waiting with Sophia's and Kate's parents. Her pulse raced. Soon they'd be talking to Ms. Fraser and there would be a million questions about Kate's accident. Inside, everyone stood up, pulling on backpacks, yawning, and yelling bye to their friends. Only Michiko was silent as she let Kate and Sophia file past her without even a backward glance.

As each student stepped off the bus, parents hugged them, collected their bags from the storage area under the bus, and headed to their cars. Michiko was the last one to get off, the Ouija board, still in her backpack, feeling like a brick. An unshakeable reminder that, thanks to it, what should have been a fun trip had cost her her best friends. She couldn't risk destroying the board and spending the coin as one should, not before it returned to the torii gate, signaling K-san was gone for good. Otherwise, K-san might linger forever. *And maybe she will anyway*, Michiko added to herself.

"Good trip?" Dad asked as soon as she got off the bus. Luckily, he'd stepped away from the other parents to help her retrieve her bag.

Michiko forced a smile and nodded. From the corner of her eye, she saw Ms. Fraser approach Kate's and Sophia's parents. "How is Mom doing?"

"Much better since yesterday, actually," said Dad. Though he looked tired, his eyes had a sparkle she'd not seen for a very long time. "I was waiting to tell you in person. The doctors think she's getting over whatever she had. She's going to be all right, Miko." Saying so, he enveloped her in a bear hug.

"Let's go home," said Michiko, burying her face in his chest. "I can't wait to see Mom."

"Don't you want to say goodbye to your friends?" Dad said, pulling away with a surprised expression.

"We said bye on the bus," said Michiko. "And I'm starving. What's for dinner?"

"Your favorite—fish tacos," said Dad, smiling. "Mom was feeling better, so she made them for you."

"Yum!" Michiko forced herself to look enthusiastic, though the mention of food made her sick.

The last thing she saw as the car turned out of the parking lot was Ms. Fraser chatting with Sophia's and Kate's parents. They were nodding, and no one looked upset. Maybe they didn't blame the school, or the Mojave National Preserve for a snake's appearance, or Sophia's tumble down the dunes, after all.

"Dad, turn on the heat please," said Michiko. "I'm freezing."

"It's on full blast," said Dad. "I was feeling cold too."

Michiko turned around to grab her sweater from the back seat and saw the unwavering outline of a lady in a kimono with a red slash for a mouth.

23

Michiko forced herself to eat the dinner Mom had made. Each bite of the tacos stuck in her throat, and she barely noticed their taste. The most important thing was that Mom, who'd been tired and sick all these months, was well enough to make dinner. Some of the color was back in her cheeks and she didn't look quite as tired. If K-san had anything to do with it, then all the pain of losing her friends might be worth it.

"So, how was the trip?" asked Mom. "You've been awfully quiet. Anything fun you'd like to share?"

Only that I played the Ouija board and K-san tried to kill Sophia and Kate. Oh, and K-san is still here, so now it must be my turn. "The Kelso Dunes were beautiful," said Michiko instead. "They're called the singing dunes, but they sounded more like a ghostly booming and wailing to me. It was legit."

The light in their dining room flickered. Mom looked up in surprise. "That's odd. I've never seen that happen before."

"Must be a glitch with the power supply," said Dad, helping himself to more tacos. "Tell us more, Miko."

For the longest time she had wanted life to go back to

normal, to sit and chat at the dining table with Mom and Dad. But tonight, she just wanted dinner to be over so she could talk to Hiro and figure out how to get K-san out of her house and her life. She kept checking her phone for a response that was certain to come soon, as it was Saturday morning in Tokyo. When Mom served the family-favorite, chocolate cake for dessert, Michiko had to force herself to keep some down, the chocolate tasting like chalk.

"You look tired, Miko," said Mom. "Dad and I will clear up. Go on up to your room."

"You look tired too, honey," Dad said to Mom, giving her a peck on the cheek. "Both of you rest. I'll clear up."

Michiko hugged them both goodnight and escaped to her room. As soon as she'd shut the door, K-san made her presence known. The chill intensified and the air got heavy. She peered at the shadows lingering in the corners. Nothing moved, but she heard that same faint muttering she'd heard before. By now, Michiko was exhausted by this spirit.

Ignoring the signs, Michiko decided to take a shower. She felt grimy, but above all she needed to clear her head. Free of distractions, the shower was one of those spots where she got her best ideas.

She ran the hot water until it fogged up the small bathroom. Once she was done, she felt squeaky clean and a lot better—even though she had no new ideas. Frankly, it was a relief to just be alone and away from the hateful looks from her two best—no, ex-best friends.

Except that she wasn't alone. She could feel the spirit's presence in the small drafts of chilly air that swept over her damp skin. She hurriedly put on her bathrobe.

"What do you want, K-san?" asked Michiko softly as she ran a comb through her wet hair. "Why won't you go? I wish you would tell me *why*. And then leave me alone."

POSSESSED

An icy breath made the hairs on the back of her neck rise as a word appeared in the steamy bathroom mirror, as if being written with an invisible finger: O-N-R-Y-O.

"What?" asked Michiko, her heart pounding. She had fully expected to see the word danger again. "Who is Onryo?"

The letters dissolved as if by magic. Michiko wanted to run out screaming but something held her there. It was the first time K-san was communicating clearly, without the board. She forced herself to listen. More steam appeared, covering the blank patch, and then another word was spelled out.

L-U-C-A-S

"What about him?" asked Michiko. The smell of shampoo was dissipating, and the stink of seaweed was growing stronger. Soon she wouldn't be able to breathe. K-san better write faster.

D-A-N-G-E-R

And there was that word again.

"*You're* the one putting us in danger, and warning us about it in advance," snapped Michiko. "That's mean!"

Suddenly, a shampoo bottle came flying out of the shower and smacked her in the head.

"OW!" said Michiko. "Stop that."

Behave. It was a raspy voice, the same one that had muttered and chanted unintelligibly in their room at the preserve.

Michiko tried to make sense of K-san's words, repeating the two names in her head to find a connection. She didn't know how Lucas was involved or why K-san had mentioned him, but a thought niggled at her now: he'd been closest to the scene during both Sophia's and Kate's accidents.

Maybe that was a coincidence. Then Michiko recalled

the look that had flashed in his eyes from time to time. The fact that he'd coolly dislodged the stone that had distressed the rattlesnake occurred to her again. But he *had* given them a good explanation for it . . . Was she just channeling her envy at him for stealing her besties again? Did K-san know this, and was simply toying with her feelings?

"No!" Michiko spoke up. "*You* behave. You've been messing with me long enough. Just stop!"

The bathroom was suddenly plunged into darkness, making Michiko almost scream out loud. She managed to muffle it by pressing her towel to her mouth. The mirror lit up, as if it were a movie screen in a darkened theater.

Lucas's striking face smiled at her from the mirror. But as she watched, his face morphed into the most grotesque mask . . . of an ancient Japanese man with bloody eyes, flesh drooping from his skull in ropes of black. A tangled bush of white hair encircled his face, and the creature's mouth started opening wider and wider in a silent scream.

Michiko scrambled backward, gasping for air. She flung open the bathroom door and staggered out, grabbing her phone from the bedside table with an icy hand. As she scrolled through her contacts and hit the call button in a panic, she stole a glance at the bathroom mirror. Lucas's face had replaced the monstrosity.

She slammed the door shut with her foot just as Hiro picked up the phone on the first ring. "I was just about to call—"

"It's Lucas! She's here, she showed me!" Michiko cut in. "His face changed. Something called Onryo . . . I don't know—"

"Slow down, Cuz!" said Hiro. "Take a deep breath and start again."

Michiko took in a ragged breath and climbed into bed.

She drew the covers over her shivering body, trying to squeeze her eyes shut so the tears wouldn't come cascading out. That she was dealing with not one, but *two* otherworldly creatures, chilled her to the core.

Within minutes, she had told Hiro exactly what had happened this morning and in the bathroom. She told him why she thought Lucas was the one trying to harm Sophia and then Kate, and that she was next. The image of him turning into that grotesque monster was etched into her mind. She doubted she'd ever forget that sight.

When she finished, Hiro was silent for a long minute. Michiko's eyes darted around her bedroom. The light was still on, and it was some comfort that she was home, in her own bed, and she could leave the lights on all night if she had to.

"What's the worst that can happen to people who don't send the spirits back?" asked Michiko.

Hiro was quiet, and she knew what that meant. It was bad. *Very bad*.

"They went mad," said Hiro, quietly. "From what I've heard, a couple of them landed up in a psychiatric facility, arguing with a ghost no one could see. But right now, we have a bigger problem. Lucas, or rather the Onryo, who is stalking you guys."

"What or who is that?" asked Michiko. "The face I saw in the mirror was a nightmare."

"I'm surprised you don't know the Japanese folklore, Miko," said Hiro. "The Onryo is a malevolent and powerful spirit. Looks like you might have summoned *two* spirits; one which warns of danger and the other which is danger personified. I've heard of rare cases where that happens. Onryo has to be sent back, but before that, send K-san back. Maybe if one goes, the other will too."

Michiko felt like hurling. *How was she going to handle this alone?*

"How dangerous is the other spirit?" asked Michiko.

"The Onryo are wrathful ghosts who are driven solely by their desire to exact revenge. Having left the mortal realm with unresolved feelings of greed, anger, or jealousy, as ghosts they thrive on their own wrath. They'll even go as far as to cause natural disasters to get their way. They are the worst of all the spirits and *very* hard to get rid of."

Michiko felt lightheaded with panic at these words. "Can you get on a plane and come here right away? I'll send you all the allowance I've saved. I really need you!"

"Unfortunately, that won't work, Cuz," said Hiro. "I'll have to do some more digging. But maybe if you work on sending K-san back, Onryo might leave too. Gray area. I don't have a lot of info."

Michiko's pulse raced as her eyes darted to the shadowy corners of the room. "How?"

"First, always be respectful. Don't ever be mean because spirits can be meaner and they're quick to anger."

"Okay," said Michiko.

"From everyone I've spoken to," Hiro continued, "only those who summoned her can send her back. This means you must get Kate and Sophia to come back to the board."

"They won't even talk to me, let alone play the Ouija board again. There has to be another way, Hiro."

"There isn't," said Hiro flatly.

"What if I tried using the Ouija board by myself to send her back?"

"No!" said Hiro. "Never attempt the Ouija board on your own. That's the first rule when dealing with spirits and cannot be broken."

Michiko bit her lip. She'd already communicated with

K-san on her own, back at the lodge. *Is that why the spirit refused to leave her? Were they tied together forever?* The smell of seaweed suddenly wafted by. K-san was still here and listening to every word she said.

"So, then what?"

"You must contact your friends and convince them to help you send K-san back. It's the *only* way."

Michiko knew that if she even mentioned the board again, there was no telling what they might do. Probably report her to Ms. Fraser, who would have a chat with Mom and Dad. *This is a disaster.*

"And last, but most importantly," Hiro said, his voice deadly serious, "stay away from Lucas, or rather, the Onryo. Seems like he's capable of way more harm than K-san. *He's* the one to watch and keep at arm's length. I'll call you back as soon as I can."

"Thanks, Hiro. You're a *lifesaver*."

"Anytime, Cuz, and please be careful."

As Michiko snuggled under the covers, an idea started to form in her mind. She would try it out tomorrow and prayed it would work. It had to.

24

Michiko bundled up in her warmest jacket and headed toward the kitchen door. It had been one of the worst nights ever, despite spending it in her own bed in her own room. Hiro's advice had pounded inside her head like a hammer that wouldn't quit. *Was Lucas really the Onryo, and what else was he capable of? Would she be able to convince her friends to help send K-san back? What if they refused?* But they couldn't —she was determined to make them see sense. The Ouija board and coin were in her backpack. No matter what, today Sophia and Kate wouldn't be able to throw her off so easily.

Mom was making breakfast, but Michiko's stomach roiled. No way could she eat a bite. There had been no news from Hiro, which meant he had not dug up any new information.

"Pancakes?" Mom asked brightly.

"Not hungry," she replied. "I'll grab something at Sophia's. We're meeting to finish an assignment."

Mom came up to her and hugged her tightly, as if to say all was well again. Her hair smelled of shampoo and crisp apples, while her clothes smelled of lemon zest. The stink of sweat and medicine were gone, and Michiko breathed in deeply. Only when something was gone did you realize how precious it was. Like Mom's health. That visceral worry, coiled inside Michiko, finally unwound. If there was *one* good thing that had come out of calling K-san, it was knowing Mom would be fine. That knowledge gave Michiko the courage to face anything coming her way.

"When will you be back?" asked Mom, pulling away.

"By lunchtime, maybe later. I'll text you," Michiko replied, hoping her guilt wasn't too obvious. It felt as if "liar" was tattooed on her forehead.

"Have a good time," said Mom, "but be back in time for dinner." She handed Michiko a brown paper bag. "Some chocolate cake from yesterday. Both Sophia and Kate love it, right?"

"Thanks, Mom!" Michiko gave her mom another tight hug and stuffed the paper bag into her backpack. Wheeling out her bike from the garage, she started pedaling hard. Sophia's house was ten minutes away and Michiko had biked there often. She always took the side streets, so there was very little traffic.

Despite it being a cold, gray Saturday, many families were outdoors putting up decorations—delicate spiderwebs, pointy witch hats, menacing jack-o'-lanterns. With everything that had been happening these last few days, she'd forgotten it was the end of October, almost Halloween! Michiko felt a pang. She, Sophia, and Kate used to decorate Sophia's house together. They would have a sleepover every Halloween night, distributing candy to trick-or-treating youngsters and then watching a scary movie. All that was out of the question this year.

Michiko was happy for the exercise and a chance to clear her head. If only she could convince the two of them that there was a more evil spirit at play—and it wasn't K-san —they might believe her and be friends again. *But did she believe K-san? What if this was another little trick of hers?* Michiko was so confused, her thoughts kept going around in circles. Another question plagued her too: if given the chance, did she *want* to be friends with Kate and Sophia again after the way they'd treated her? One summoning gone wrong, and their friendship had fallen apart like a tower of Jenga tiles. *What kind of best-friendship was that?*

The screech of tires and a blasting horn jerked Michiko out of her reverie. A black SUV was inches from the front tire of her bike, so close that she could reach out and touch it. She hadn't even realized she was in the middle of a crossroads. If the driver hadn't stopped, she would have been smeared on the road like raspberry jam.

Stunned, Michiko blinked at the driver, who rolled down her window and stuck out her head. "Look where you're going, kid!" The woman looked shaken but concerned. "If I hadn't stopped in time..."

Michiko got off the bike shakily. "Sorry, and thanks."

The woman nodded and drove away, leaving Michiko to wheel her bike to the curb. Her legs felt like cooked spaghetti. She reached the sidewalk and plopped down.

A man who'd been playing with his kids on the adjoining lawn came up to her. "Are you okay? Would you like some water? Or maybe I can call your parents?"

"I'm fine now," Michiko said. "I, er, wasn't paying attention. It's my fault—" A sudden jolt took her by surprise; for the briefest moment, her body felt as if it were on fire. She'd felt the same passing sensation when Sophia had fallen, and when the snake had threatened Kate. It couldn't be a coincidence. But, was this K-san's warning or the Onryo's?

Her head reeled with questions, but she forced herself to

smile at the waiting man and got onto the bike. She rode carefully the rest of the way to Sophia's house, only to find a giggling Kate and Sophia putting up Halloween decorations without her. Michiko's first instinct was to turn around and go back before they saw her. But she forced herself to pedal forward, trying to let go of her anger and jealousy. They had to work together, and she didn't have a choice. *I also have to warn them about Lucas*, she reminded herself, so they could stay alert when he was around.

Michiko took out the cake from her bag and approached them, her stomach gurgling with anxiety. "Hi!" she said, wheeling her bike up to the lawn. "May I join you?"

Sophia's smile slipped. Kate looked shocked.

"I can't believe you're here," said Kate. "I thought we'd made it clear that we didn't want to be friends with you."

The Kate Michiko once knew spoke in sentences that ended in a question. As if she was never sure of herself or what she was saying. Now she sounded strong and determined, even if mean and downright rude.

"Mom sent her chocolate cake," said Michiko, holding up the bag. "Can we talk inside for a few minutes, please? I can say hello to your parents, too," This last comment she addressed to Sophia.

"They've gone out for the day," said Sophia, looking over Michiko's head. "They'll be back home later."

No one moved. An awkward silence ballooned between them.

"Let's go inside," said Michiko, dropping all pretenses. "This is really important, and you *have* to hear me out."

"We don't *want* to," said Kate. "Go away."

"What she said," Sophia added. "We have nothing to discuss."

Michiko closed her eyes and took a deep breath, hoping

she could get through to them without losing her temper or having to beg. Neither option sounded pleasant. She opened her eyes again. "I spoke to Hiro—my cousin—last night. I have a plan to make this right, but I need your help. He also told me a few things I didn't know before, and it's important that you know, too."

"*Fine*, we're listening," said Sophia, crossing her arms over her chest.

"Inside," said Michiko, looking around, now nervous by habit. "I'd rather we didn't have anyone eavesdropping."

Sophia and Kate exchanged a look, which did not include Michiko. Without a word in response, Sophia swiveled on her heel and went inside, with Kate in tow. Michiko gritted her teeth and followed them in.

25

The familiar smell of cilantro-laced guacamole lingering inside the house brought a lump to Michiko's throat. They'd spent so many days doing homework here, and so many nights gossiping and trading secrets. They'd watched movies, painted their nails, and talked about nothing and everything. That was all gone now, thanks to K-san.

Again, Michiko offered Mom's cake to Sophia and Kate, but they both shook their heads. Michiko put the brown paper bag on the kitchen table and sat down. She figured she'd get right to the point.

"According to Hiro, all the people involved in summoning a spirit have to come together to send it back. Whether you like it or not, you'll have to help me."

"Hah!" said Sophia. "We did! We tried *so* hard, but it didn't work. You don't know what you're doing."

"I'm not touching that board again," said Kate, glaring at Michiko.

Michiko looked from one mutinous face to the other, crushed. "Fine, then I guess K-san will linger here forever. She may even try to harm us again."

"You mean harm *you*," said Sophia shrewdly. "You've not had your turn, and you're scared. Serves you right!"

Michiko took a deep breath and swallowed, trying not to cry. This was so much harder than she'd thought it would be. Neither of them could see reason nor could they empathize with her. And she didn't dare try to do it alone, not after Hiro's warnings. It was at the tip of her tongue that a more malevolent spirit than K-san was involved, and, somehow, Lucas too. But she decided to hold her tongue again. If one spirit had them this scared, two would tip them over the edge. She'd have to break it to them gently.

"I've had my turn," she said bluntly. "I was almost run over as I was biking here today and could have died if the driver hadn't stopped in time."

There was a flash of concern in Sophia's eyes, but Kate's remained cold and hard. Could Michiko blame her? Facing down a venomous rattlesnake would change you forever.

"But you didn't, and here you are," said Kate. "You really think that telling us a sob story will get us to play that horrible game again? No way."

"Why are you being so stubborn?" snapped Michiko. "We were friends once, remember? I only want the best for both of you."

"You didn't treat us as your best friends when you kept your mom's health a secret from us," Kate snapped back. "Nor did you think about us when you forced us to play so you could ask about your mom. You were only thinking about yourself then, and not our safety, so don't you dare lie about your intentions now."

She had a point, but so did Michiko. "You two wanted to know about Lucas," she said. "You asked questions, too!"

Before long, they were screaming at each other, when suddenly there was a loud crash. A glass jug of water on the far counter now lay on the floor, smashed to pieces. No one had to wonder whose doing it was. The three of them lapsed into shocked silence as the room quickly turned icy, as if someone had thrust them into a refrigerator.

"Here we go," said Kate in a small voice, clinging to Sophia. "She's back, and she's never going to stop haunting us!"

Michiko looked around the room. *Which spirit could this be?* "K-san?" she said. "What are you trying to tell us? Please be clear."

They sat still for as long as they could, but nothing moved in response. Kate plopped onto a chair, white-faced. Sophia sat down, holding her head in her hands.

"We're never going to be free of her, are we?" she said. "She'll keep coming back to haunt us all."

"She's restless and there's something she wants to tell us. We have to give her a chance to tell us through the board and then ask her to go back. It's the *only* way."

"So, we're stuck. Having to do what *you* want," said Kate, hatred in her eyes. "You're a terrible person, Michiko, and I wish I'd never met you."

Michiko had no reply. She was resigned to being their punching bag if it meant she could keep them safe and see this through, once and for all.

"You said your parents will be out late, right?" she asked Sophia.

Sophia looked at the floor, and then at Kate. She didn't reply, but she didn't need to.

"You were lying," said Michiko simply.

"They're not back until tomorrow, and Kate and I are having a sleepover," said Sophia stiffly. "Our neighbor Ms. Ohi will check in with us a few times, and we have to call her in the night, and first thing tomorrow morning."

"A sleepover for two," said Michiko with a shake of her head, more mad, than hurt. "Fine, I'm out of this circle. I get that, and I won't try to get back in. Let's just finish this and neither of you need to speak to me ever again. Tell your parents and Ms. Ohi I'm staying for the sleepover too. I'll tell my mom the same thing. We'll see what K-san has to say and then send her back, even if it takes all night. Okay?"

No response. For a long minute, all three of them remained silent, staring at the shattered jug on the kitchen floor, a puddle of ice forming around the shards.

"Let's do this," said Sophia finally. "After this, you leave us alone."

"What she said," Kate echoed.

26

Michiko pedaled back home to get her stuff for the sleepover and to tell Mom and Dad. She'd done this so many times, there was no protest. They didn't even ask if Sophia's parents were home, and Michiko didn't volunteer that information. It wasn't lying if no one asked, right?

Right.

The good thing was, Hiro would be awake at the time they'd set up the board. She'd be able to text him for advice if she needed it. She was sending K-san back tonight, no matter how long it took, or what the dangers.

At dusk, Michiko biked back to Sophia's house with a large Tupperware container full of noodles Mom had packed for their dinner. There'd been no point going early. Her ex-friends hated her now and the less time they spent in each other's company, the better for them all. A chill hung in the air, unusual for this time of year and especially in California. Michiko knew the reason and shuddered.

By the time she arrived, Sophia's house looked ready for Halloween, with graves and cobwebs illuminated spookily by well-placed lights. They'd be facing the *real* thing today. The irony of the situation didn't escape her.

She knocked on the door and then shoved her freezing hands into her pockets. After a long wait, Sophia opened it. It almost felt deliberate. Did Sophia hope Michiko might give up and go away if she had to wait too long? She couldn't help but recall the time, just a few weeks ago, when Sophia had seen her pedaling up the driveway and was waiting on the porch with a smile and a hug.

"Hi," said Michiko, stepping inside.

"Hey," said Sophia in a voice that held politeness but no warmth.

Kate was on the living room couch, already in PJs, with a large bowl of popcorn on her lap. It was sure to be caramel flavored—Kate's fave.

They ate dinner in silence, each of them staring at their cell phones or their plates. The shrill ringing of the landline made Michiko jump. It was only the neighbor, Ms. Ohi, checking up on them. She talked so loudly; Michiko could hear her clearly from where she was seated.

"Yes, we're indoors and we're safe," Sophia said to the old woman, holding the receiver away from her ear. "Michiko is staying over too. We'll be fine. I'll call in the morning. No, we haven't invited boys over, only a ghost. Yes, I was joking and I'm sorry. We're *thirteen*, Ms. Ohi, and very responsible. You don't have to worry about a thing!"

She rolled her eyes after she'd hung up and sat down. Kate laughed. Michiko almost smiled too because Sophia had spoken a truth most people wouldn't take seriously. If this weren't their last evening together, maybe they could have tried to revive what had been lost. But their friendship was already dead and lying somewhere in the Mojave Desert.

While they were clearing away the dishes, also silently, Sophia's phone pinged with an incoming text. She texted back with a smile playing on her lips, which grew broader when her phone started ringing. "Hey, Lucas!" she said in a sing-song voice.

An icy finger traveled the length of Michiko's spine as she watched Sophia chat with Lucas. *When had they exchanged numbers?* Fear gripped her when she thought of Lucas, and Hiro's warning to stay away from him. Next to her, Kate drew the robe of her PJs tighter around herself to protect against the growing chill in the kitchen, her eyes glued to Sophia.

After two minutes of gushing and giggling, Sophia threw the cell phone on the table with a flourish and pumped her arm in the air. "Eeeeeep! Lucas said he might drop by for some hot chocolate later this evening! *Neither* of you is allowed to tell Mom."

"You go, girl!" said Kate, imitating Sophia's fist pump.

"NO!" said Michiko. "Call him back and tell him he can't drop in. We must take care of K-san tonight. There can be *no* interruptions, *especially* not from Lucas."

Sophia glared at her. "Who do you think you are, telling me what I can and cannot do in my house?"

"The person you never have to see again if we send the spirit back tonight," said Michiko.

"She has a point . . . you don't want to worry about a ghost following you when you're getting to know Lucas better," said Kate reluctantly. "Just tell him to drop by tomorrow. We'll get rid of them both tonight—her and K-san."

Michiko ignored the burning in her gut at these horrible words and started setting up the board. Sophia's shoulders slumped as she picked up her cell phone and texted furiously. Then she threw the phone on the table with a clatter.

It was already dark outside by the time the three of them took their seats around the board, but they had the entire night ahead of them. The wind had picked up. A tree branch scraped against the window.

"Let's get this over with," said Sophia as the clock struck nine. "If we can get K-san to go back, *you* can leave, too." She turned to Michiko with a cruel smile that didn't reach her eyes. "No need for you to spend the night here."

27

"Kokkuri-san, I know you're here," said Michiko, starting off differently this time. "What's the danger you've been warning us about?"

They were seated around the low coffee table in the living room, with their fingers on the coin. Michiko had set up the board and placed the coin on the letter R, where it had last been, when she'd packed up the board.

Please let this work, thought Michiko. *Don't let me make this worse somehow.* She called the spirit again, feeling the anger and resentment coming from Sophia and Kate in waves. She focused on the board, on the spirit, and on staying calm.

"Answer me, Kokkuri-san," said Michiko in her most authoritative voice.

The temperature in the room dropped, and a low muttering came from the far corner. The lamps flickered and the door to the kitchen banged shut. She was here, and she sounded agitated.

Michiko glanced at the clock, wondering how long it would take them to get the answers they needed and send her back. She willed the coin to move with all her heart and soul. It didn't.

"If you have nothing to tell us, go back to where you came from," said Michiko. "We do not need you here."

Nothing.

They took turns talking to K-san, telling her to go back, and the night started unraveling around them. A china figurine on a shelf fell and smashed to bits. The room alternated between warm and frigid. The spirit's muttering grew louder and then dimmed. She was playing with them, circling them, keeping them on edge, and Michiko hated her with all her heart. This wasn't a trickster, but a mean and evil spirit, playing a game of cat and mouse with them.

"It's almost midnight and clearly this isn't working," said Sophia, her face blotchy with anger. "You're just making things worse!"

"*I* should have followed my instinct and not agreed to play," said Kate. "I *knew* this was a bad idea and now we're at it again."

"Stop whining!" said Michiko. "Let's finish what we started and then we never have to talk to each other again. I feel there's a reason this is happening, and the spirit just needs time. Okay?"

Suddenly, the coin moved. They all sat up straighter. It was spelling out a word. Michiko fully expected it to spell "danger" again, and again—but it did not.

"Onryo?" said Kate. "Who's that? Do you know anyone by that name, Michiko?"

Michiko hesitated. Should she tell her friends that it meant a super-evil and wrathful spirit? In her mind it could very well be the devil! The last thing she wanted was for one of them to have a meltdown. She didn't know if she'd have the strength to go on by herself—not after Hiro's warnings.

She opened her mouth to answer when, suddenly, everything seemed to happen at once.

The doorbell rang.

All the lights went out.

A piercing shriek reverberated through the living room.

Kate screamed and Sophia let out a terrified whimper. Michiko barely contained her groan. They'd both whipped their hands off the coin and were hugging each other tightly.

"Who's that?" Kate asked in a shaky voice. "And why is that spirit screaming? I want to go home!"

"Kate, don't leave me!" said Sophia in an equally shaky voice. "I'll get the candles. Don't answer the door just yet."

Michiko turned on the flashlight on her phone. They all watched as the coin started zooming across the board, all on its own.

D-A-N-G-E-R

D-A-N-G-E-R

D-A-N-G-E-R

"Do something, Michiko!" wailed Kate. "Don't just sit there."

Michiko took a deep breath and said nothing. There was nothing she *could* do until Sophia returned.

Once the candles were lit, the girls put them all around the room. Pockets of shadows flickered inside, and the calming scent of vanilla filled the air. Except that there was nothing calming about being without power and having a stranger knocking at the door.

Creeping to the window, Michiko peered out carefully. All the other houses on the street were dark too. She looked behind her. The candles were no match for the darkness.

A shadowy figure stood on the doorstep. "Someone is

still outside, Sophia," Michiko whispered. "Do you think it's your neighbor?"

"Hey, Sophia!" said a familiar voice. "Open the door. I'm freezing out here."

No way.

"It's Lucas! I told him not to come, but I guess he couldn't stay away from me," Sophia said, nervously. "I better let him in. We'll have someone to help in case anything goes wrong. I bet he could take on K-san and win!"

"No!" said Michiko as Sophia headed toward the door. "Don't open the door and don't let him in."

"What?" said Sophia. "The poor guy is freezing. I *have* to let him in."

There was a chill gust of wind, even though all the windows were shut. Two candles went out. Angry, unintelligible muttering reverberated from every corner of the room.

"Um, guys, the board's gone mad," Kate squeaked.

They gathered round the Ouija board, where the coin was skating around on its own, still spelling out just one word over and over again.

N-O

N-O

N-O

"*Don't* let Lucas in," said Michiko.

"Why?" asked Sophia. "Because he chose me and Kate over you? We were supposed to meet tonight to go to the cemetery. He said he had a surprise and I'm *not* letting you ruin it."

At that, Michiko finally figured out the last piece of the puzzle, and the picture looked ominous. She had to tell them—it was now, or never.

"Because *he* is the danger K-san has been warning us about."

28

"What? You're jealous and making up all these lies!" said Sophia.

"How can you say that?" said Kate, frowning. "Lucas is always the first one to help us out. He even tried to help Sophia when she fell."

"That's because *he's* the one who creates the problems in the first place," said Michiko. "I think K-san hasn't gone back because she's protecting us all. I just figured it out when you mentioned the cemetery."

Lucas pounded on the door with his fist. "Let me in, guys, I'm freezing. I thought we'd take a walk and see the Halloween decorations. And don't forget the surprise I've planned for you both!"

Michiko moved to the door. "Go away, Lucas! We're not letting you in."

There was a long silence.

"Are all the doors locked?" Michiko whispered. "Back door, too?"

In the flickering light of the candle, Sophia turned pale.

"I-I don't know. I took out the garbage before dinner and I can't remember."

"Go quick and check, while I keep an eye on Lucas. Please, just for tonight, trust me again and do as I say," said Michiko, looking from Sophia to Kate with pleading eyes.

More than ever, she was now convinced that K-san was doing them a favor by hanging around. She had no idea what Lucas would do, but she was convinced there was something very wrong with him. He wasn't the concerned friend he was trying to portray. She glanced at the board. The coin had stopped moving and was now resting on the letter O.

"Be right back," said Sophia as she zipped into the darkness toward the kitchen.

Kate relit the candles that had gone out. "You really think it's Lucas?" she asked, coming to stand beside Michiko. "He's been so helpful ever since the trip."

"Who was right behind Sophia when she fell?" asked Michiko. "Didn't she tell us it felt like someone pushed her? What if that had been Lucas and not K-san?"

Kate's eyes widened. "How do you explain the snake? Lucas couldn't have put it in my path. That's impossible."

Michiko thought back to the scene, which was so vivid in her mind. "No, but he might have disturbed the snake on his way up. And then, when you were frozen, he kicked the stone from the top, hoping to scare the snake into striking you. He said it was an accident, but I'm sure he was lying. I believe Lucas is possessed by Onryo—a malevolent and vengeful spirit."

Kate was silent for a long time. Then turning to Michiko, she said, "I think you may be right. You guys couldn't see it because I was blocking the view, but after a few minutes, the snake was about to retreat into a hole. It was just backing

POSSESSED

away when that stone fell. Then its tail starting vibrating, and that rattling sound . . ." She wrung her hands together. "I'll never forget that sound or that forked tongue, flicking in and out, for as long as I live."

"So you agree with me?" said Michiko.

"Where's Sophia?" said Kate suddenly. "She's taking a very long time to lock the back door."

They both peered out the window. There was no one at the front door. Lucas had disappeared.

"Sophia!" they yelled in unison and raced toward the kitchen. Michiko had a terrible feeling they might be too late.

As they burst into the kitchen, she knew she was right. The back door swung open in the chill breeze, and the kitchen was cold and empty.

"She's gone!" said Kate in a whisper. "Lucas?"

"Who else?" Michiko replied grimly. *Why* had she let Sophia go to the kitchen alone? They should have all gone together. There was safety in numbers, always.

"They won't be far," said Kate. "If we run, we'll catch up to them."

Cemetery, a raspy voice whispered.

They both jumped and turned around to face K-san up close.

Michiko got a good look at the trickster spirit, who had a glow around her. She was a wizened old Japanese woman in a black kimono with a broad yellow waistband, her hair in a bun. The black eyes were without pupils. Her smile was still that bloody slash that gave Michiko the creeps. She was sure she'd have nightmares about this face for a long time to come.

"GO!" said K-san, urging them forward with her thin arms, over which the kimono sleeves flapped.

"She's right," squeaked Kate. "Lucas was going to take us to the cemetery down the road tonight. I'm sure that's where they're headed. Oh, I hope Sophia is all right!"

Michiko and Kate raced down the familiar road to the last place Michiko wanted to be this late at night, but their friend was in danger. The entire street and neighborhood was unseasonably cold. If it weren't supernatural forces at play, Michiko didn't know what it was.

"Sophia!" yelled Kate as soon as they burst through the side gate, which was always unlocked, into the darkened cemetery. "Where are you?"

A sickle moon slid through tatters of cloud as Michiko's gaze roved over the tombstones standing guard over all those dead bodies laid to rest in the ground. She shivered and wrapped her arms around her.

"Sophia! Call out if you can hear us!"

No response.

"Lucas!" said Michiko. "If you've done anything to harm our friend, you'll have to answer to us. Show yourself!"

For a long minute, nothing moved. Only the wind sighed through the trees. The cold was so intense that Michiko's teeth chattered.

"Please, Lucas," begged Kate. "Where's Sophia?"

There was a slight movement to their right. Kate moved closer to Michiko and slid a cold hand into hers just as Lucas stood up from behind a large tombstone. His eyes shone bright red, and his mouth was curved in a smile. He looked nothing like the sweet, good-looking boy who had charmed them all. There was no sign of Sophia.

Kate took a step back, but Michiko held her ground. She hoped K-san had followed them here. That she would continue to protect them as she had these last few days.

"Where is our friend?" said Michiko, her voice quavering.

"Safe for now," said Lucas. "You should go back home. I'll bring her back after I take one thing. Her soul."

"What?" Kate screamed.

"Onryo took mine a while ago," said Lucas, coming closer with a swagger. "At this very cemetery. It's simple. If I want mine back, I have to give him another. It's taken a while to gain Sophia's trust, but it's been worth it. Soon I will be free of the nightmares and Sophia will have to find the next victim. It might even be one of *you*. You'd like to help a friend, right?"

"I don't understand," moaned Kate.

"You don't need to," said Lucas. He was suddenly in their face, teeth bared, eyes like burning embers fanned by the wind.

Again, Kate shrank back, but Michiko took a step toward Lucas. "You don't scare me," she said.

Lucas opened his mouth to laugh and the stink of something dead blasted her. She stood her ground, trying not to hurl. Her skin burned and the night seemed to turn darker. Now she knew why. It was the proximity to Lucas, and Onryo.

"Give her back right now or else—" said Michiko.

"Or else what?" sneered Lucas, cutting her off. "You'll call on that pathetic old ghost to come rescue your friend?"

Immediately, the air grew heavy with the stink of seaweed, and seconds later, Kokkuri-san materialized beside them.

"Yes, she will," said the old woman in a raspy voice. She followed that up with a volley of Japanese words that sounded like she was yelling at him or cursing him.

Kate and Michiko moved back as the spirits started

circling each other, eyes locked. The ground turned white with frost and their breath came in puffs.

Clearly visible, K-san didn't look half as bad as what she was facing. Lucas, possessed by the Onryo, now looked like some creature from a horror movie. His face was gaunt, almost skull-like and his flesh seemed to sag. His hair had turned white and stood on end around his face like a halo, even as his red eyes glared at K-san. Around them, the cemetery seemed alive as wind whipped through their hair. The stink of rotting seaweed was now interlaced with the foul smell of burning flesh.

"Let's find Sophia while they're busy," whispered Kate to Michiko, both running toward the tombstone from where Lucas had emerged.

"Please let her be safe," Michiko muttered under her breath as they peered behind each tombstone. She had a horrible feeling that they might already be too late.

29

They found Sophia crumpled behind a gray, cracked tombstone, her face white, her eyes closed.

They both ran to her and hugged her limp body. Thankfully, her breath was still fogging in front of her face.

"Sophia, wake up!" said Kate, gently slapping her friend's face.

But Sophia did not stir.

"What if we're too late?" said Michiko as she tried to wake her up.

Less than half an hour ago, Sophia had been yelling at her. She would give anything to have her friend awake and yelling again. Instead, she was slumped on the ground, unconscious, her hair matted with leaves, face coated with dirt.

"She wouldn't stop screaming, so I had to silence her somehow," said Lucas, suddenly coming up behind their crouching figures. "At midnight, I will go free, and she will be under Onryo's spell." He laughed long and loud, and Michiko pressed her hands to her ears to block out that terrible sound.

"K-san, help!" wailed Kate. "We're sorry to have doubted you."

Sophia opened her eyes just then. She was shivering so hard that she could barely speak, but she heard Kate and added her own plea. "Help us, K-san. We need you . . . I'm sorry too."

Michiko looked at her friends. For the first time, they fully believed in K-san and the power of the Ouija board. She added her own plea to the spirit. "K-san, don't fail us now. Please!"

K-san shuffled out from behind the tombstones, and Lucas cackled maniacally. Goosebumps rose on Michiko's arms at that sound.

"You think an ancient woman is any match for the devil? Go home, old woman, before you get hurt."

Suddenly, there was a loud boom that rocked the whole cemetery, making it glow as if hit by lightning. Michiko, Sophia, and Kate huddled together, mesmerized by the scene unfolding before them.

When the darkness returned, Lucas lay on the ground writhing and shrieking. K-san had him pinned with her tiny foot clad in a high-heeled wooden sandal. Bending over, she reached into Lucas's chest and started pulling something out. It looked like a black rag, but as more of it emerged, it took shape. By the time she was done, she was holding a thin, wizened old man by the throat. Cowering beside an unconscious Lucas, he looked starved, beaten, and very angry.

The old man howled, and the cemetery echoed with his cry. The hairs on Michiko's arms stood up, and she clutched Kate and Sophia tighter.

"You will leave these children alone," said K-san, dragging the old man so close that their noses almost touched. "They are under *my* protection."

The old man squirmed, but K-san's grip around his throat tightened. "I was *here* first," he said, saliva frothing at the sides of his mouth. "This boy's soul has been mine for a while. He disrespected my grave and angered me. All my life, I've been pushed around in a country I wanted to make my home. I couldn't do anything while I was alive, but now I can, by commanding souls! This one is too weak, and it's time for a change. I want another soul, who will cause the suffering *I* felt during my mortal days." His fiery red eyes fell on Michiko. "I can feel the strength of your spirit. I should have focused on *you*."

Kate moaned and Sophia gripped Michiko's hand so tightly, she thought the bones would shatter. She wanted to hurl, or cry, or pass out.

Suddenly Sophia dropped to the ground and picked up a large stone. "You come anywhere close, and I let this fly," she said in a shaky voice.

Hiro's words came back to Michiko, like a bolt of lightning illuminating the night sky—the solution to all their problems. "Violence or anger is not the answer here," Michiko whispered to Sophia and Kate. "Can you trust me one last time and follow my lead?"

They nodded and Sophia dropped the stone. Michiko started walking and the others followed. They approached the spirits—Onryo, cowering, yet defiant, and K-san, regal and horrific with the slash for a smile. The three of them bowed as low as they could, staring at the ground, their hands folded.

"Please accept our humble apologies, Onryo and K-san," began Michiko. "Lucas was wrong to disrespect you and, if he were awake, I know he would be very sorry too." Michiko peeked at the spirits. The old man had stopped squirming and was listening intently. K-san's smile was even wider. Michiko turned her eyes away before her dinner landed on her sneakers. "Kate, Sophia, and I were also wrong to summon you, K-san. I can only say that my worry for my mother made me thoughtless. If you forgive us, we will forever be grateful and will always remember you." *That last part was true*, thought Michiko. No way was she forgetting this nightmare.

A chuckle made Michiko look up. The Onryo was grinning—and grotesque as it was, with his flesh hanging over his mouth as if he were melting, it was better than an angry spirit.

"This one's strong *and* smart," he said, looking at K-san, who had released him from her grip. "Respect was all I wanted when I was alive and all I need now."

The Onryo took a step toward them. Kate and Sophia gasped aloud and immediately clapped their hands over their mouths; Michiko shuddered involuntarily. *What if this was just a ploy and he decided to possess one of them?* K-san made no move to stop him, watching him speak with a strange expression on her face.

In one slick movement, the Onryo was face to face with Michiko. His foul odor assaulted her nose, and it took every bit of willpower not to run. His red eyes bored into hers and, for a few seconds, the world around her dimmed—turned black. Her skin burned as if on fire.

When the blackness lifted, Michiko found herself looking into soft brown eyes. The flesh on Onryo's grotesque face seemed to shrink back, slowly replaced by the face of a middle-aged man who looked infinitely sad. The Onryo gazed at her a second longer and bowed to her, too. "I will not harm any of you, but I make no promises for the future. I am what I am."

Then he took a step back and vanished in a puff of smoke.

Immediately, Kate and Sophia both fell on Michiko and hugged her so hard, she couldn't breathe. But there was still K-san to take care of.

"Thank you for watching over us," Michiko said to K-san.

"Thanks," Sophia and Kate echoed.

For a minute, K-san said nothing, her black, pupil-less eyes boring into them. Suddenly, she jabbed each one of them in the chest. Michiko gasped as the icy finger burned her flesh even through all the layers she wore.

"You will *never* play the Ouija board again," said K-san in a cold voice. "This is not a game, and we spirits are sick of being disturbed for silly and unimportant questions. Is that clear?"

They all nodded.

"And now I'm leaving," said K-san, "so you don't have to pull out the board again and ask me to go. Just remember to destroy it, and spend, or give away the coin—it's tainted. Goodbye."

A red torii gate suddenly appeared behind her, shimmering in the darkness. K-san walked through it and disappeared. The gate faded after a few seconds and the cemetery lights flickered back on. The chill dissipated and the air was warm again.

"Let's go home," said Sophia.

"What about Lucas?" said Kate. "Looks like he's still out cold."

"We'll bring him with us," said Michiko.

30

They were all gathered in Sophia's living room, hands wrapped around mugs of hot chocolate.

"What happened to you?" Michiko asked Lucas. "How did you become possessed?"

Lucas hung his head in shame, looking into the depths of his cup and swirling it around. No one said anything, and only the ticking of the clock broke the silence. *Somehow, he looked smaller, less confident than he'd seemed before,* thought Michiko. She'd never been into him, but it looked as if Sophia and Kate were over their crushes, too. They weren't hanging on to his every word, nor did they look at him adoringly, the way they used to.

At last Lucas spoke, his eyes moist with tears. "Being new at this school, I wanted to fit in with the cool kids and be a part of Sasha's group. They insisted I go to the cemetery on a dare. It was scary, and I did something silly. I kicked the crypt in the center of the cemetery and ran back. And then the nightmares started."

He put down the mug of hot chocolate and wrapped his arms around himself to stop from shivering, despite the warmth of the living room. The terror in his dull blue eyes was very real. He looked more like a lost boy than the cool kid Michiko had seen strutting around the school halls and in the desert. She picked up a blanket from the sofa and tossed it to him. Lucas gratefully wrapped it around himself.

"Michiko has a theory that it was you who pushed me," said Sophia.

"And disturbed the snake," added Kate.

Lucas looked at them both, shame written all over his face. "You have a clever and caring friend. And yes, it was me. Something made me do it even though I resisted so hard."

"Onryo," said Michiko.

Lucas nodded. "I'm so sorry, you guys. If anything had happened to you both, I could never have forgiven myself. It was horrible—the nightmares, the craving for rotten food, and the unexplained bursts of rage. Mom and Dad were so worried, they were discussing sending me to a psychiatrist for help. I couldn't tell them anything. They wouldn't have believed me."

Michiko shook her head in sympathy. "I remember you eating that rotten baloney sandwich."

Lucas gave a grim smile.

"And then the spirit gave me the answer: get me another soul, and I will release you," said Lucas. "Apparently it likes young souls, like ours, to feed on. And that's when I started being friends with others. Somehow, Sadia saw through me. She thought I was odd and questioned me so many times, I had to keep my distance before she figured out that something was wrong and told Ms. Fraser or my parents."

"Why not pick on Sasha?" Kate demanded. "It was because of him and his group that you got into this mess in the first place."

"I tried," said Lucas, staring into the depths of his hot chocolate. "We went out late that first night at the preserve. I was hoping to take him to a secluded spot and let the Onryo do the rest. But Sasha thought I was *into* him. After politely telling me that he was not into me and that I should leave him alone, he ditched me before I could corner him. I didn't want any more trouble, and didn't want him spreading rumors about me, so I went after you guys."

"So that means K-san hung around only to keep us safe," said Kate. "The snake flying backward makes sense now."

"That's not all that happened," said Michiko.

They all looked at her quizzically.

"Kate, just listen to how confident you sound now," said Michiko. "And you, Sophia, you're so popular. And I know Mom's going to be fine. There was some good that came out of the Ouija board for all of us."

Sophia scooched closer to Michiko and Kate did the same. "We're sorry for being so mean to you," said Sophia with tears in her eyes. "Despite all that, you looked out for us, for our safety. You could easily have left me in the cemetery, but you didn't. You came looking for me."

Michiko shrugged.

"We're so lucky to have you as a friend," said Kate. "And I'm so ashamed of the awful things I said to you. I don't know what came over me..."

"You can blame the Onryo for that," added Lucas. "He brings out the meanest and most cruel side of the person he possesses, as well as anyone around them. I should know. He's been in my head for three months now."

"Thanks, guys. We're good," said Michiko. "But there's one last thing I have to do, and then let's never speak of summoning spirits again."

With a flourish, she tore up the Ouija board into forty-eight pieces, remembering how Hiro did it after every calling, and put it back into the bag. Tomorrow, she would bury it somewhere safe so no one would stumble upon it. The coin would have to be spent. She couldn't go all the way to Japan to get rid of it, so she'd just drop it into a coin tray at the local 7-Eleven. The main thing was that it couldn't stay with her. She wanted nothing to do with spirits anymore. Onryo's last words echoed in her head. 'I make no promises for the future. I am what I am.'

Michiko was suddenly exhausted. All this had happened in less than a week, and yet it felt as if she'd been battling evil spirits for months now. Tomorrow she would tell Hiro that she'd finally done it, but not tonight. Tonight, she would have fun with her friends as they chatted about everything and nothing. Things were back to normal.

EPILOGUE

At the local 7-Eleven, Raina picked up a jug of milk and a loaf of bread. The supermarket was farther away, and Mom was too tired to take the car out. Raina had offered to get the basics from the store if she could also get some goodies for herself. The Harry Potter films were airing during the Christmas holidays, and Raina was out of snacks.

She grabbed a bag of pizza-flavored chips and her favorite candy along with the milk and bread and plunked them down on the counter. The man behind the till, an Indian dude, was watching a Bollywood movie on the small TV inside his booth.

"How much for all this, please?" asked Raina.

The man rang up the order with one eye still on the movie, which had an exciting car chase and lots of explosions. "Ten dollars and five cents, please," he said.

Raina glanced at the ten-dollar note in her hand. If she didn't buy the candy, she had enough change. But if she did, she was short. Then she noticed the coin tray in front of her. "May I take five cents from here? I'm a little short."

The man grunted as Raina rooted around. Her eyes fell

on an odd coin. It looked foreign, and the wording was in Japanese. She had the strongest urge to pick it up and pocket it rather than give it to the man behind the counter.

"I've changed my mind," said Raina. "I don't want the candy anymore."

The man canceled the sale of the candy, and Raina paid the bill with a little change left over. She dutifully dropped a couple of coins in the coin tray and picked up the odd one, the one with the Japanese writing. "May I have this?" she asked. "I collect coins."

"Okay," said the man, now clearly wanting her to go away.

Raina walked out with the milk, bread, and chips. On the way home she passed a trash can. Under it, almost out of sight, was a half-eaten sandwich that was rotting and had been forgotten long ago. Raina dropped to her knees, fished it out, and munched it all the way home.

If you liked this story, please consider leaving a review on Amazon or Goodreads. I would very much appreciate it, and your review will help other readers find their next scary read!

Buy the other two books in the series now, to enjoy being **WARNED** *and* **HAUNTED!**

AUTHOR'S NOTE

There was a time when I loved horror movies. A watershed moment was when I watched the movie *Evil Dead* and completely lost my appetite for hardcore horror. However, I still yearned for the thrill, the visceral reaction of not knowing what is going to pop out from behind a closed door, or the next paragraph in a story!

Fast-forward to the present, when I decided to combine my love of Asian mythology, the horror genre, and writing scary stories. It started with a fantasy adventure about Tara, which spanned the three books in the Tara Trilogy: *The Third Eye*, *The Silver Anklet*, and *The Deadly Conch*. I'm thrilled that WARNED—*The Astrologer's Prophecy*, HAUNTED— *The Cursed Lake*, and POSSESSED—*The Ouija Board*, making up the Eerie Tales from the East series, are now out in the world!

POSSESSED is the third instalment in the series and revolves around the Ouija board, the subject of an interesting article in *Smithsonian Magazine*. According to historian Robert Murch, who has been researching the Ouija board's origins, its name came about in a serendipitous way

POSSESSED

that warned its players: "Sitting around the table, they asked the board what they should call it; the name 'Ouija' came through and, when they asked what that meant, the board replied, 'Good luck.'" It grew in popularity in the 1920s because people, in uncertain times, wanted to find answers or commune with the dead using DIY oracles.

It's no wonder that this activity spread through the world, and the idea of Kokkuri-san (an animal spirit) grew popular among school-age kids in Japan, who would invoke this spirit to ask who loved them or if they'd be rich and famous. Another article goes on to say that, at one point, this game caused such mass hysteria among Japanese youth that it was banned. But as we all know, banning only makes the banned object all the more popular (I'm still waiting for one of my books to be banned!).

In addition to the adventure surrounding the Ouija board, one among the scariest urban legends in Japan, I also wanted to explore the themes of friendship, belonging, acceptance, as well as forgiveness and loyalty. In short: the gamut of emotions and needs that kids and adults face, with or without stubborn spirits who refuse to leave.

Recommended Reading:

Fiction:
Amari and the Night Brothers by B.B. Alston
Wonder by R.J. Palacio
Real Friends by Shannon Hale and LeUyen Pham
Onibi: Diary of a Yokai Ghost Hunter

Non-Fiction:
Dictionary for a Better World: Poems, Quotes, and Anecdotes

from A to Z by Irene Latham, Charles Waters, and Mehrdokht Amini
Social Skills Activities for Kids: 50 Fun Exercises for Making Friends, Talking and Listening, and Understanding Social Rules by Natasha Daniels LCSW

<u>On Mythology :</u>
Mythopedia: An Encyclopedia of Mythical Beasts and Their Magical Tales by Good Wives and Warriors
The Book of Mythical Beasts and Magical Creatures by Stephen Krensky
Myths, Legends, and Sacred Stories: A Visual Encyclopedia by Philip Wilkinson
The Atlas of Monsters: Mythical Creatures from Around the World by Sandra Lawrence and Stuart Hill
The Book of Yokai: Mysterious Creatures of Japanese Folklore
Tales of Japan: Traditional Stories of Monsters and Magic
Japanese Legends and Folklore: Samurai Tales, Ghost Stories, Legends, Fairy Tales, Myths and Historical Accounts
Yokai Attack!: The Japanese Monster Survival Guide

ABOUT THE AUTHOR

Mahtab Narsimhan has had four careers in her lifetime. Writing is her fifth and favorite. She has worked in the hotel industry, the credit card industry, as well as the recruitment industry (general and IT).
Mahtab immigrated to Canada in 1997 and started writing in 2004. Her debut novel, *The Third Eye*, won the Silver Birch Fiction Award in 2009 and she hasn't looked back since. Mahtab is deeply committed to representing diversity in her stories. For more information, please visit her website at www.mahtabnarsimhan.com or connect with her via Twitter @MahtabNarsimhan.

Also in the Eerie Tales from the East series:
Warned: The Astrologer's Prophecy
Haunted: The Cursed Lake

More Books by Mahtab Narsimhan :
(Available anywhere books are sold. Please see her website for more information.)

The Tiffin
The Tiffin Audiobook
Mission Mumbai (Teachers' Pick)
Embrace the Chicken
Genie Meanie
Valley of the Rats

Project Bollywood
Careful What You Wish For

Picture Books:
Looking for Lord Ganesh
You and Me Both

ACKNOWLEDGMENTS

I'm grateful for the support of my friends and family as I continue to publish this series. A special shout-out to friend and writer Lee Edward Fodi, who has been a tremendous help on this journey and whose son inspired the character name, Hiro. Thanks to Amber Cowie, Diana Stevan, Karen Dodd, Rae Knightly, Shoshona Freedman, and Sonia Garrett, who continue to help me swim indie(p) waters!

Thank you to amazing friend and writer, kc Dyer. You keep me motivated, and sane.

This one has been a hard one to write! Thank you, Cristy Watson, for all your hard work on this novel.

Last but certainly not the least, thank you, Dear Reader. I would not be here without your support.

WARNED
THE ASTROLOGER'S PROPHECY

EERIE TALES FROM THE EAST

MAHTAB NARSIMHAN

WARNED
THE ASTROLOGER'S PROPHECY

Chapter 1

THE LINE outside the astrologer's tent snaked through the village fair—long and sinuous. I wondered if he was that good. Not that I believed in any of the rubbish superstitions or fortune- telling that seemed to be the case here.

My phone rang half-heartedly. I grabbed it and pressed talk, afraid I would lose the weak signal if I moved.

"Hey, Lee!" I said. "Miss you, man. How's Delhi?" Lee was my best friend and miles away. I should have been there with him, or he should have been here. I tried to ignore the pang in my gut when I thought of two weeks in this remote village without a friend.

"Miss you too," he said. "Delhi seems weird without you. Where are you again?" His voice crackled and broke. The signal was so terrible I was scared I'd lose him.

"Tolagunj," I said. "Small village up north. My grandfather is some bigshot here with the title of zamindar. Something like a head honcho with lots of land." I swatted a large wasp that buzzed by. My fingers touched the EpiPen in my pocket and my heartbeat slowed. As long as I had it with me at all times, I was okay. No wasp could hurt me.

"What are you planning to do there for two weeks?" Lee asked.

"Probably die of boredom," I said, gazing at the villagers milling around food stalls, the cows and goats wandering by, the amateur game stalls. "I brought boo—" I started to say when someone snatched the phone out of my hand.

I whirled around and there he was—a weirdo in a black kaftan and a fancy turban of colored beads that covered his face. He gripped my arm and dragged me into the tent, despite the grumbling villagers in line.

"How dare you?" I squeaked, my eyes darting around the bare tent. "This is child abuse!"

"I'm an astrologer and I see grave danger in your aura," he said. The beads swayed and tinkled as he spoke. "Leave now or you'll die a horrible death!" Stinking of sweat and sandalwood, he leaned close. "This year the wasps are the worst I've ever seen. Enough of them sting you and you're dead," he hissed.

I stared at him, aghast. "Who told you I'm allergic to wasps? They do nothing to me." Yet he'd spoken the truth. Probably a lucky guess.

"The nearest hospital is fifty kilometers from here," he said in a whisper. "Want to take your chances?" The heat in the tent was stifling.

"Give me my phone," I said, jerking my head toward his hand.

"Will you leave if I do?" asked the astrologer.

"Who are you to tell me what I should do?" I said. "And no. I won't." I shuffled backward out of the tent and bumped into a villager, who grumbled loudly.

The astrologer followed, his black eyes boring into mine from behind the curtain of beads. Barefoot, he stood there and surveyed the line of waiting customers. Sweat pooled at the base of his neck, which he wiped away with a grimy hand and then muttered under his breath, making the complaining villager blanch.

This guy was a weirdo and a bully. He'd probably seen me swat at that wasp when I was talking to Lee and predicted that I feared them to get me to pay him. I'd read somewhere that most fortune-tellers had excellent powers of observation. There was no way I was parting with any money for this fraud, even though he'd made a lucky guess.

"I say this for your own good," said the astrologer. "Why do you want to die young?"

"You're making this up just to scare me," I said, stepping out of reach before he grabbed me again. "You saw me swat that wasp earlier. It's summer so there will be lots of them around. You're a fraud."

"Only one way to find out," he said. "You're in grave danger here, and I have warned you. Your parents will lose their only child."

An electric current jolted through me. *How did he know this stuff?*

"Phone!" I said.

The astrologer slapped it into my hand, muttering under his breath. If he thought I'd react the same way as a villager, he was sadly mistaken.

"I don't believe your predictions," I said. Though it felt like an army of mice were running up and down my spine, I wouldn't let him see that he'd rattled me. It would only make him spout more crap or lucky guesses.

His laugh was chilling. The beads in his headdress clattered together softly. "Then stay, and you'll see that I'm right.

Your poor parents." He dismissed me with a wave of his hand and turned to a waiting villager.

I looked around for Mom and Dad. I had to try once more (and only the billionth time!) to plead with them to let me stay with my friend Lee in Delhi, while they were volunteering as doctors in Rajasthan. This desert state was suffering from serious drought and illnesses among its farmers. They'd already told me Nana was a technophobe and there'd be no Wi-Fi at his place. I was going to be bored out of my mind in Tolagunj. They couldn't expect me to read books for two entire weeks. Unless I died before that. I tried not to think about it as I hurried through the fair, looking for Mom.

I found her talking to a man wearing a white dhoti-kurta and a snow-white turban, with a face like a prune. When I walked over to her, she put an arm around my shoulders. "Avi, this is Mr. Venkat, the head of the panchayat in Tolagunj. The panchayat settles disputes in the village, much like a court in the city," she added when she saw my puzzled expression.

"Um . . . okay," I said, not really interested in anything except that she'd let me go back to Delhi.

"I threw up on him as a kid," Mom continued, laughing. "Mr. Venkat, this is my son, Avijeet."

TMI.

Mr. Venkat gave a hearty laugh, which sounded totally fake. I managed a weak smile.

"I have to talk to you, Mom," I said. "It's urgent."

She gave me the stink eye. "Excuse me," she said to Mr. Venkat. "I'll be right back."

As soon as we were out of eavesdropping range, she shook her head as if she already knew what I was going to say. She was right. "No, Avi, we're not leaving. You will stay here with Nana. It will be a pleasant change of pace for you, and good for him too. He's been very lonely since Nani died."

"So *you* spend time with him," I snapped. "Let me stay with Lee. Please, Mom. This place feels weird—people are lining up outside an astrologer's tent to have their fortunes told!" I refused to tell her about my brief encounter with him.

"The villagers are very superstitious," said Mom. "Don't hold it against them. I know Nana did not want us to come, but I think he needs his family. Besides, we're only staying a week in Rajasthan and the second week we'll all be together. I'll show you my favorite hikes around here. We'll have fun, I promise."

"Mom, any house without Wi-Fi and cell coverage is child abuse," I said. "I can barely get one bar on the phone here."

She laughed. "Sue me. Meet us at the car in twenty."

I wandered through narrow aisles between stalls set up in the village square. It was loud and noisy. Smells of fried food, parched earth, and manure filled the air. So unlike the city, where it would have been the smells of coffee, petrol, and garbage. I missed the white noise of traffic and was already homesick.

Villagers, dressed in bright clothes with the men sporting colorful turbans, called out to me to buy food or play a game. I ignored them all, trying not to feel too sorry for myself. If I really thought about it, I guess I could put this time to good use and finish writing my scary story and read a ton of books.

A plump vendor with a double chin was selling *gulub jamuns*—fried sweets dipped in sugar syrup. A cloud of flies perched on the wire dome covering them, but not a single one had got through the mesh. *Good!*

"I'll have five, please," I said, pulling out a ten-rupee note.

The vendor slipped tongs under the dome, plucked five golden-brown balls and put them into a cone made of dried banana leaves. He handed me the change.

I walked slowly, savoring the rich sweetness in my mouth. A prickle at the back of my neck made me pause. Someone was watching me. I glanced around, but no one seemed to be looking my way. The villagers wandered in and out of stalls, chatting or playing games, while kids whooped and darted around in the late afternoon sunshine. Cows with tinkling bells chewed the cud. Stray dogs scrounged in piles of garbage beside the stalls.

Was the astrologer stalking me? But he was nowhere around.

A shadow between two stalls moved. A young girl was sweeping up the garbage into a handheld pan with a small broom. She was dark-skinned and wore a heavily patched kurta-pajama with a white dupatta draped over her head. Red bangles on her arms clinked softly as she swept, her eyes riveted to the sweets in my hand.

She looked away when she saw that I'd noticed her. She was so thin her cheekbones stood out like twin peaks on either side of her nose. The mouthful I swallowed almost stuck in my throat.

"Hello!" I called out, walking over with a smile.

She stood up, clutching the broom to her chest. Her eyes were a pale gray.

"What's your name?" I asked.

Her eyes strayed to the sweets in my hand and then she looked away.

"Do *not* talk to an untouchable!" someone behind me bellowed. "Don't you know it's bad luck for you and for the village? We only speak to give an order. Otherwise, keep your distance and ignore her. It is our way."

I whirled round as this ugly word—"untouchable"—bounced in my head. Mr. Venkat stood there, his moustache quivering indignantly. Mom had warned me that the villagers were not only superstitious but also old-fashioned. They still believed in the outdated caste system. Yet, to hear the head of the panchayat speak it so casually and with such conviction made me sick. And furious.

HAUNTED
THE CURSED LAKE

EERIE TALES FROM THE EAST

MAHTAB NARSIMHAN

HAUNTED
THE CURSED LAKE

Chapter 1

JONAH BROUGHT the axe down with such force that the block shattered. A large piece of wood splashed into the water, sending ripples toward the center of the lake. Only a patch the size of a rowboat, beyond the buoys, remained undisturbed. Oily calm.

Strange, thought Jonah as he massaged his aching back. He shielded his eyes from the glare of the sun and stared at the spot for a while longer. If only he had time for a quick dip, he would have a chance to investigate. Was there a current in that section which kept the water so calm when the rest wasn't?

A gust of breeze wafted toward him, bringing a myriad of smells —water, sunshine, fresh grass, damp wood, and an underlying tinge of something putrid. An animal had probably died in the forest on the far side of the lake. He'd have to ask Mom about it and get the caretaker, Frank, to find it and bury it. The smell would get worse as the weather grew warmer.

Jonah stood at the edge of the water. The oily, calm patch had disappeared. A wind ruffled the surface of the lake, and the sun poked golden fingers into its sandy bottom, pockmarked with algae-covered rocks. How awesome would it be to swim all day, then lie on the grass with a book—

"Jonah! Stop dreaming and hurry. I need help with the cabins."

Summer had just begun, but Mom's voice was already tinged with exhaustion and impatience. This was their first year running Camp Sunny Acres since they'd bought it last fall. If they didn't do well this season, it would all be over.

"Coming!" he called out.

As Jonah stacked the wood in the shelter beside the lake, he breathed in a lungful of resin and something earthy, like mushrooms. Birds squawked raucously overhead, playing tag. If only he could be a real camper and look forward to a summer filled with nothing but swimming, sports, crafts, and reading. But since Dad died two years ago, life had changed for the Anders family. His last summer had gone by in a whirl of bagging groceries and babysitting. They had needed the money. Running a camp this year had to be better.

Stay positive, he reminded himself. Dad would have wanted him to be brave and look after Mom. He was the man of the family now, and he had to stop feeling sorry for himself.

Mrs. Rastogi, the cook, whom they had inherited when they bought Sunny Acres, walked toward the cafeteria with an armload of groceries. Plump, with a kind laugh and salt-pepper hair—which she wore in a plait down to her waist—she was, hands down, the best cook ever.

"Let me help," said Jonah as he hurried up to her.

"Thank you, Jonah," said Mrs. Rastogi, letting him take a few bags from her arms. "Ready for the campers? It's going to be non-stop for the next two weeks."

"I know," said Jonah, trying not to sound mournful.

"What's the matter?" said Mrs. Rastogi.

Jonah shrugged as they trudged up the pathway between the cabins.

The place looked rundown, and in need of repairs and a fresh coat of paint, but it already felt like home. Would the campers like it enough to come back the next year? Could he and Mom make a success of Camp Sunny Acres, or would they have to pack up and leave in the winter? The questions, like a cloud of mosquitoes, wouldn't stop bugging him.

"There's so much to learn and do out here," said Jonah. "I hope we have a great season. I love this place already and don't want to leave."

"None of us know what fate has in store for us," said Mrs. Rastogi softly. "You come to me if you need any help or if something is bothering you. Okay?"

Jonah flicked a glance over his shoulder at the lake. The sun was high in the sky and its surface glittered like a million diamonds. A breeze cooled his warm face. Did he dare ask her about that weird patch in the water? Would she think it was his imagination and laugh at him?

"Sure," he said. "Thanks, Mrs. R."

They'd reached the cafeteria and entered through the back door into the kitchen. He placed the groceries carefully on the table.

"Anything else?" he asked her.

"Just this," said Mrs. Rastogi, taking an ice-cream sandwich from the freezer. She handed it to Jonah. "Finish that *before* you meet the campers, or they'll all want one before lunch."

"Thanks," said Jonah.

He took the long way back to the camp office, strolling beside the lake as he bit into the cold sandwich, enjoying the sweetness on his tongue. There was a loud honk and the crunch of gravel. The busload of campers had arrived.

They'd need help to register, find their cabins, and settle in. Then a tour of the camp, so they knew where everything was before heading for lunch. *Better hurry.* If Mom had to call out twice, there'd be fireworks before Canada Day.

A wave tiptoed stealthily to shore. Jonah paused, watching, as it sidled up to the sandy bank and spent itself in a hiss of foam. His heartbeat quickened. There were no fish in this lake. No boat had gone by, nor was there any breeze right this minute. So where had the wave come from?

Just as he turned to run to the camp office, someone whispered, so softly he wasn't sure if he'd heard it or imagined it.

"*Jonah.*"

Milton Keynes UK
Ingram Content Group UK Ltd.
UKHW021705100624
443998UK00038B/564